REN: The Arrival

C. M. Garcia

Copyright ©2023 By Christina M. Garcia

All rights reserved, including the right to reproduce this book or portions thereof in any form whatsoever without written consent from the author, except in the case of brief quotations embodied in critical reviews and certain other noncommercial uses permitted by copyright law.

ISBN: 979-8-218-19121-4 (Paperback)

Although this novel is inspired by true events, it is a work of fiction. Names, characters, places, and incidents either are the product of the author's imagination and are used fictitiously. Any resemblance to actual persons living or dead, businesses, companies, events, or locales is entirely coincidental.

Book Design, Cover Design and Illustrations
By C. M. Garcia

For sales and other information email: friendofren22@gmail.com

First Printing Edition 2023

Published by Christina M. Garcia
www.TheInkCrusader.com
Printed in the U.S.A

Share with the Lord's people who are in need.
Practice hospitality.

Romans 12:13

This book is dedicated to everyone who
had a part In pulling me out of the darkness.
Thank You.
-Ker

Chapter 1
The Arrival

November 1, 1888

It was a beautiful morning in Puebla, Mexico, when Julia Reyes stirred to awaken from sleep in her bed, alone in her room. As she sat up and her feet touched the wooden floor before finding her sandals nearby with her toes, her right hand moved from the bed sheets to her stomach just below her belly button. Her eyes not yet opened as she touched her stomach, she remained stuck in thought about the dream she just had and knowing it was not the reality she was currently living.

In her dream, she was a mother. A beautiful baby girl with a bounty of brown hair on her head, round brown eyes, and a round chubby face with squeezable cheeks was in her arms. Ten fingers and ten toes and probably close to ten pounds of pure love filled her arms and her heart with joy. (A dream of a daughter she longed to have, she just spent the last 8 hours having, and didn't want it to end as she kept her eyes closed.) As Julia savored that last vision of a daughter, her eyes slowly opened, slightly watering from the emotions she felt, both joy and sadness.

"It was just a dream." She reminded herself. "This *pansa* right here feeds only you right now." She joked as she looked down, grabbed it with two hands and gently shook it.

She looked down at her feet as she sat up on the edge of her bed and took a deep breath before standing up into her sandals. She never liked the feeling of the bare floors of her house, no matter how often they were cleaned. As she arose she turned to face her empty bed and reminded herself, *Javi will be home today. Let's get to work; it's going to be busy at the shop, and you're short handed, especially with the festivities in town.* This was her attempt to motivate and distract her thoughts from her dream.

Javier was her husband of 5 years now and was away on one of his trips overseas. It had been 5 years of joy, growing together, and, of course, sorrow. Though they had successful growing businesses together, they had not yet been blessed with a growing family. Pregnancy did not come easy for them, and it was just this past summer that they had experienced a miscarriage after years of nothing. It was a heartbreaking experience after euphoria filled their souls when they found out they were finally expecting. It was something neither of them would have been able to cope with if it hadn't been for the comfort of their family and undying faith that their dream of becoming parents would still come when the time was right. *But when will that be?* Was the thought always in the back of their mind.

Julia and Javier both came from decent sized families. Javier was the oldest of 4 sons, and Julia the second oldest of 5 brothers and sisters. But Julia was soon turning 33 and her husband was 4 years older. They felt like time was getting short, and the gentle nagging from Julia's live-in mother-in-law for grandchildren wasn't helping. But as long as she kept nagging, strangely, it kept hope alive that at least this parent believed it would still happen for them. That was "the upside" they would tell each other with a hint of sarcasm.

"It's not like we're not trying!" was Javier's go-to answer for his mother, Maria. After her irritating repetitive rundown of "old wives" tricks of getting pregnant, suggestions of prayer to St. Gerard, and even some herbal remedies of her own Huasteca-Mexican mother's recipe book that she often referred to those "cures" that she kept in her possession, since her own mother's passing not 4 years ago. This is how she kept close to her mother now.

"Mama Happy knows, *Mijo*. She was a healer in her village, remember? She could fix anything! You don't become known as a healer if you don't heal," Maria would reply often while shaking her mother's book in his direction. Javier would just turn to walk away, rolling his eyes so his mother wouldn't see.

On the other hand, Javier was traveling often too, so that didn't help their situation for those windows of opportunity. At least he was able to escape his mother's lingering requests for those grandbabies. Julia didn't travel along with Javier often. For the most part, Mama Maria did her best to hold her tongue when it came to Julia's infertile situation for the most part. Maria would be supportive in helping care for Julia like a daughter, who was always staying behind to keep things running at their shop in the plaza and little *posada,* as they nicknamed their home. Regardless, there was no lack of love or intimacy between Julia and Javier. A baby just was not an appearing by product of that union. However, baby making practice was also getting overplayed at the same time between the two. Javier would be turning 37 that coming spring.

As Julia finished dressing for the day, she braided her thick brown hair into buns with bows to look festive. She was tucking away a couple strands of gray hair behind her ear as she vowed to have a wonderful day and to give her best service to every customer coming into the shop. Surely, they would be excited to celebrate this day of remembrance, *Dia de los Muertos*. She took a quick glance at a small mirror on the wall, smiled, and grabbed her bag as she exited her room. Julia followed the hall to the large central kitchen, where Maria was busy cooking away usually. Though they called the home little *posada* it actually had many rooms and belonged to the King of Spain before losing the territory in the war. In its most basic description, it was more like a hotel. Gifted to Javier's grandma on his father's side, the family did their best to make use of the property by filling it with family and extended family over the years. Once it seemed that the family growth was slowing followed by some even moving away, it made sense to use it as a hotel for travelers instead and which did benefit the family financially. Julia enjoyed having guests. It was their presence in the halls, dining rooms, and patios that eased the thought of loneliness that would try to fill her mind.

"*Aye*, Maria, you're cooking up enough tamales for an army today!" Julia teased as she entered the kitchen.

"Well, all my boys are going to be here today, *Mija*. Better to have too much than too little!" Maria reminded her.

She then motioned to Julia to sit at the table as she brought her a plate of eggs, beans, and fresh tortillas for breakfast. Julia thanked her and the kitchen helper who had just brought her a cup of coffee, as she ripped a tortilla to dig into her meal. Maria brought a second plate to the table for herself to join her daughter-in-law for breakfast. Once they came close to finishing their meal and talking about the plans for the day, Julia shared her dream with Maria, describing the baby in her arms she kept visualizing in her mind. She spoke slowly, with deep breaths for pauses, hoping to not get too emotional as she shared it. Maria listened intently, and her eyes became glossy with emotion as a crooked, shaky smile crossed her lips. As a tear escaped Julia's eyes when she finished the story, she quickly looked down at her plate and tried to wipe it discreetly with her finger before Maria could see. The loss of the baby that summer was also painful for Maria. The notice seemed to happen just as soon as the happy news had even arrived.

Maria only had sons, making Julia was her first "daughter," and the hope for a granddaughter was a dream of hers too. As Julia wiped the little tear from her finger on her skirt and brought her hand back up to the table, Maria reached for it. She gently tapped Julia's hand with care, squeezing it hard enough for her nails to slightly dig into her palm as they both sat there in silence. Their minds focused on the same thing with hope for that "one day."

"What a beautiful dream, *Mija*. I cannot wait to meet her too." Maria said with encouragement and uncertainty at the same time. She stood with her plate in one hand and grabbed her apron with the other to wipe her own eyes as she turned around and headed back towards the stove.

Julia finished her meal and polished off her coffee, kissed her mother-in-law on the head, and told her she'd see her later for dinner when Javier returned. Maria had become a concrete mother figure to her over the years, not only because she lived with her and Javier but also because of a lack of a relationship with her own mother. Julia spent most of her childhood living with her grandmother and grandfather in their *casita* in Puebla, while her parents lived in Mexico City with her brothers and sister in a large *hacienda*. Julia was also the first granddaughter to her grandparents, Aurora and Antonello. With her parents' constant, rocky relationship growing up, she just felt more stable staying with her grandparents full-time opposed to just weekend visits anymore. Of course, Grandma Aurora didn't mind one bit. They lived life simply, maybe not on the wealthy side when it came to money like her parents, but there, it was rich in love and life. Julia just loved the closeness she experienced living with her grandparents, but they, too, had now passed, not long after her marriage to Javier. It was as if they stayed on earth just long enough to see her new life begin.

      Making her mile walk into the town square, Julia's mind became distracted from her earlier emotions and now filled with the anticipation of the day. *Dia de los Muertos* was one of the biggest days of the year for business in their shop, and the fact that it had been established for more than a few years now, their customer base was at the highest it's ever been. Javier had hoped to be there to help her, but since his trip got off to a late start, his return would be affected as well. Julia didn't mind the challenge though. She loved busy days in the shop and loved seeing all the new and familiar faces she had come to know over time. Deep down, she had a prayer for help in the shop. Her other part-time helper who often came to the shop to work, had been sent home to rest since she was feeling ill the day before. Today, she would be alone.

As Julia got closer to the shop, she noticed a young woman nearby who seemed a bit lost.

"Good morning, *Señorita*, how are you today?" Julia greeted the stranger as she headed towards her direction.

She looked to be in her later teenage years, as thin as a rake, wearing a brown, raggedy dress and worn sandals. Her face was clean, and her hair was neatly braided in two long braids that came down her chest, her hands clutching a bag she held at her midsection. The young woman's face turned from worry to optimism when she saw Julia smiling at her as she came near.

"Good day, *Señora*." The girl quickly replied. "I am actually looking for some employment at the moment."

"Wow! Well, that is great to hear. It's like you heard my prayer right in time! I could use some help today in my shop for the festivities," Julia exclaimed in relief. Julia continued, "If you'd like to get started right away… I'm Julia, and this is my shop just across the street." She motioned at the brightly painted building ahead of them. The young woman beamed with excitement. The girl's arms came down from their anxious position, and she swung her bag across her shoulder as if she were ready to go.

"I guess I was in the right place at the right time. Thank you! Yes, I'm ready to work." She squeaked, as she quickly followed Julia, who didn't pause for more than a second as she kept heading for her shop.

    When they arrived at the shop, Julia had just grabbed the handle as she unlocked the door, paused, and looked at the girl and realized her error. With her keys in hand, Julia brought them up to her heart and spoke.

"I'm kind of distracted today, I'm sorry, I didn't even get your name." She said apologetically.

"I'm Angela," she quickly replied.

Julia closed her eyes and bowed her head just slightly and gracefully.

"Angela, thank you for being here today. Please come in," she instructed, gently smiling as she opened the door for her to enter, bell ringing overhead.

Inside the shop, there were many beautiful things, toys, gifts, candles, blankets, and collectibles for kids, adults, and everyone in between. In the corner, a large suit of armor on display stood, complete with helmet, boots, and a sword at its side, as if it were being held by the statue's hand. Angela was so taken aback by its size that she grabbed the strap of her bag across her chest and looked at it in confusion then at Julia.

"It's Javier's, my husband. He's always bringing home these silly things from his trips people seem to give him. He said it's to scare off the demons, but I remind him that that is what this is for," she said, pointing at a beautifully carved crucifix hanging nearby. "His father made that, not long before he was taken from Javier's mother and brothers." Julia bowed in its direction, motioned the sign of the cross over her heart, and kissed her hand quickly as she refocused and continued to open the curtains of the shop.

As the day progressed, Angela was quiet for the most part. She worked hard completing any task Julia came up with and smiled sweetly at any customer that came in. Many of them smiled back in return, but once they saw Julia's familiar face, they would dive right into conversation. Customers looked over the new items Javier had brought back from his last trip overseas that were delivered from their storage in Veracruz earlier that week. The shop wasn't large, so they would display the goods from Italy slowly. It was important to not take up too much space for the locally made items their store sold from various crafters and artisans in their home country. Javier and Julia had been so blessed in finances from their family's rich history in Puebla that growing the community in support of the sales for the locals was their biggest priority. Candles, figurines, and bundles of sage were flying off the shelves that day, along with plenty of other items customers found to complete their *ofrenda* presentations for their loved ones that had passed on.

As 5:00 approached and business slowed down for the day, Julia made a stronger effort to learn a little more about her new employee.

"Do you have any nice plans for tonight, Angela?" she asked.

Angela, who didn't exactly have a look of anxiousness to leave the store and kept finding anything to do, dust, or arrange to stay longer, quietly replied, "No, *Señora*. Actually, I'm not sure where I will go from here."

Without much hesitation, Julia, who had already suspected some sort of uncertainty for this girl's situation from the moment she saw her that morning, responded with, "Great, you can join me at my home tonight. I would love to introduce you to my husband who will be arriving soon so he can meet the girl that saved me today from this restless day of work! Please, won't you join us for dinner?" Julia inquired pleasantly.

Angela beamed with a smile and quickly replied, "Yes! Thank you. I would love to meet your family to tell them it was YOU that saved me today, offering this work in your lovely store."

Julia laughed and shook her head as she headed for the broom for a final sweep of the store. Angela closed the curtains and grabbed her bag that she had placed behind the counter that morning, stopping to look at the painting that hung on the wall. A massive tree with sprawling branches, green leaves, and the sunlight in glittering gold paint peeking from behind it was framed in a dark wood. She seemed to get lost in the art when Julia came beside her.

"I painted that, before I met Javier, of course." Julia shared. "It was a tree that was not too far from my grandparents house where I grew up. I loved climbing trees as a young girl, and trees were the first thing I learned to draw from my grandfather after he taught me to climb them," she laughed. "Painting is something I do for fun when I'm alone sometimes. When I'm here, I look at that tree and just get lost in memories of me and my grandparents together," she finished with a smile. She then held out a bundle of folded up cash and motioned for Angela to take it. Angela smiled, carefully took the money from Julia's hand, and put it in her bag. Together, they left the shop and headed for Julia's home.

By this time, the plaza was bustling with activities. Families gathered to watch the performers and musicians. Laughter and greetings between family and friends were everywhere you looked. Julia motioned toward the street leading out of the plaza where they had met that morning.

"This is the way home," she instructed Angela, while nodding her head in the direction to go. "We need to get out of here before sundown and things get too exciting." She joked.

As they departed from the plaza and the sounds of music became more distant, they passed the nearby cemetery where many had gathered to pay their respects as well. Julia glanced toward the tombstones decorated with candles and flowers and turned back to Angela.

"Javier's father would have been buried there, but since his untimely death, Maria decided to have him cremated since my mother-in-law always said that she'd be cremated and tossed among the fish of the lake. She said he can wait for her there for now," Julia commented as she tried not to laugh passing the cemetery. Cremation was something Maria's ancestors had done instead of burials.

"What happened to you father-in-law, if you don't mind my asking? Sorry if it's a sensitive subject…" Angela asked cautiously.

"Oh, no it's fine. I never met my father-in-law, but Javier and his mama always speak so fondly of him I feel that I did know him. Unfortunately Rolando, Javier's father, was murdered on his way home from work one day." Julia recalled. "A desperate man stabbed him in the chest, robbed him, and left him for dead. That man ended up taking his own life in shame right after Rolando's, since some people nearby had seen what he had done. Javier was only 15 years old at the time too. So sad to lose a father so young," she noted.

Angela just shook her head in disappointment, looking down at the dirt road they were now on. As she then looked up ahead, she could see a large hacienda they were approaching with a sign nearby that said *Casa de los Reyes*.

Julia stopped and turned to Angela and warned, "Probably best to not bring up Rolando at dinner until they do. I can be a little bit of an over-sharer, and my husband is more of the private type," she said with a nervous laugh.

Angela gently smiled and nodded, "Of course."

At the front of the house, Javier's horse and carriage were being led away by one of the groundskeepers of the *posada*. The front door was still ajar, undoubtedly by Javier, who must've just walked in. Julia excitedly picked up a little speed hurrying into the house to greet her husband, motioning to Angela to hurry along with her. As she entered the front room, Javier had just finished an embrace with his mother as he set down one of his bags. Hearing footsteps coming in the door he turned towards Julia and smiled upon seeing her face. They headed for each other with open arms. With one arm at Julia's waist and the other hand behind her neck pulling her close, he lovingly kissed his wife as she gripped his brawny arms and pulled him close as well. After one long passionate kiss, he rested his forehead on hers and they whispered how they missed each other. Angela then caught Javier's eye.

"Oh, a guest! Who is this, *Corazon*?" Javier inquired.

Julia quickly adjusted her top that had crept up as she had just embraced her husband who was notably taller than she. "Oh Javier, this is Angela. She saved me at the shop today, thank God. Letty was sick, and she must've heard my prayer," she explained. She then motioned and directed her husband to meet the young woman that stood before him. Javier reached out his hand as Angela held out her own.

"Angela, thank you for assisting my wife today. Looks like you were in the right place at the right time!" he said as he carefully shook her dainty hand.

"That's what she said this morning to me!" Julia interjected.

"Nice to meet you, *Señor*. Your wife has been a generous employer and host to me today, and I thank you for allowing me into your home tonight," Angela shared as she bowed her head.

"The pleasure is ours, Angela. Welcome, come in please, let us take your bag or something." Javier offered graciously as he looked around for a suitcase, assuming she'd be staying the night as well.

"Thank you, *Señor*, I only have my small bag here; I can manage," she quickly replied as she pulled on the strap of her purse across her chest.

"I see," Javier commented, with a slight tone of concern.

"Angela will be joining us for dinner with your brothers tonight, *Amor*. She didn't have plans and I just enjoyed her company so much today, I insisted she come and be our guest," Julia announced.

Angela stood there smiling when she noticed Maria, who'd also been standing nearby, peeking into some luggage her son had brought home. Maria caught her eye and quickly dropped a cloth suspiciously covering one of the luggage pieces and walked towards Angela.

"Good evening, *Mija*, I'm Maria," she said as she greeted Angela with a kiss on the cheek. "I'm Jaiver's mama. Forgive my children for not introducing me. Come, let me show you to the kitchen and washroom so you can clean up for dinner. I'm sure my son needs to take a minute to get settled and cleaned up for dinner as well. Javier's brothers are in the dining room already. Let's go meet them," Maria instructed as she led Angela out of the entry room with a hand at her back, gently pushing her along.

Julia just motioned in confirmation that Angela, who was looking back at her as she navigated down the hall, should go along with her mother-in-law and mouthed, "I'll be right there!"

Julia, who also noticed Maria suspiciously looking at the luggage, started up.

"What did you bring home this time, Javier?" Julia asked with a tone of irritation, motioning at the luggage piece covered in a cloth.

"*Amor*, it's a gift!" he said nervously with a smile.

14

"A gift for who? Me or something someone gave you again but you're saying it's for me?" she gently interrogated as she picked up his coat from the chair with her eyes locked on his.

Javier then picked up the cloth to reveal the item hidden underneath; a little wooden cage with a tiny brown bird bouncing along the perch inside. Light coming from the setting sun outside through the still open door seemed to set tiny specks of gold and red color alive on the bird feathers like glitter and velvet.

"A bird, Javi? What's this?" she asked as she approached the cage to get a closer look, and a tiny smile broke across her lips and softened her face.

"Yes. It's a wren. It's a symbol of rebirth," he said optimistically, hoping Julia would quickly come around to accepting this gift. "But yes. It was a gift to me, but I thought it was a sign for both of us when the woman told me its symbolic meaning," he added.

Julia lifted the cage by the handle on top, bringing the wren closer to her eyes to speak to it.

"Hello, *Chica*. You're so quiet I wouldn't have guessed you were the one hiding in there, did you have a long trip?" Julia asked the wren as she now carried it away down the hall to their room. Javier picked up the rest of his bags and followed behind her.

    As the family gathered in the dining room later that night, it was as if they were the only ones in the house. Almost every guest had gone out for the festivities in the plaza for the evening, and the staff had also been excused to join their families as well. The seven of them later moved outside to enjoy the large outdoor patio to finish their after dinner coffee. In the distance were faint sounds of music coming from the plaza.

"Well, that's it for me," Tomás heaved, as he stood taking his last drink of coffee. Tomás was the youngest of the brothers and had been eyeing Angela all night. He had finally grown restless getting no reaction from her with his countless passes he tried to make at dinner. The twins, Arsenio and Adriano, took turns kicking their little brother under the table with every come-on he attempted, but Angela was oblivious to it all.

"Goodbye, Mama," he said as he kissed her on the head. "I told my friends I'd come down to the plaza tonight for the music. So I'm off."

"Okay, *Mijo*, see you later," Maria replied to Tomás with a yawn.

Julia and Javier said their goodbyes to Tomás, hugs and all. With that, the twins agreed that it was time to go too, stood, and offered to walk their mother to her room before taking off to their own gatherings near town as well.

As the family departed, Julia and Javier looked at each other in a sort of mental agreement. "Angela, shall we show you to your room for the night?" Julia proposed.

"Oh no, thank you, *Señora*. You've done enough for me tonight. I should be going as well." Angela quickly replied.

"No, no, no. We insist. It is late and too dark for you to be walking home now. We won't be able to sleep tonight not knowing if you got home safely. We have plenty of rooms here available to you," Javier interrupted.

Angela then stood as she placed her cup and plate on the side table by her chair.

"No. Really, I cannot stay, but I am thankful for your offer," she repeated as she looked at the couple seated in front of her. "I'm afraid I haven't been completely honest with you today," she continued with a deep breath.

Javier and Julia looked at her with confusion and quietly listened for her to go on.

"You see, I don't actually live here in Puebla. I actually came a long way to see you both today to bring you a gift," she confessed.

As she turned to reach into her bag still across her body, a blinding light then filled the room. The couple squinted and attempted to shield their eyes with their hands, as their hearts began to pound in fear. When the light subsided, a large, beautiful angel stood in little Angela's place.

    The angel, who resembled Angela with her long brown hair in braids and olive skin, was breathtaking and intimidating at the same time. She stood taller than Javier and was no longer the frail-looking teen Angela was. This angel was well built. Muscular arms, legs, neck, and even her feet. She had a full face, strong jaw, and perfect skin with brightly-colored hazel eyes. Her wings, even larger than she, framed her body head to toe in pearl white brilliance. The dress she wore was similar to what Angela had on earlier. However, this one looked brand new and well put together. When Javier and Julia's bewilderment lessened and began to process what was before them, they then noticed that there in the angel's arm was a baby. She was dressed in white clothes with golden trim designs, round face, and squeezable cheeks. It was the baby of Julia's dream from that previous night!

Julia gasped as she covered her mouth. Javier's hands were at her shoulders as if to protect his wife during the angel's transformation. They both looked from the angel's face to the baby's, and the angel finally spoke to break the silence.

"We have seen your struggle and heard your prayers for a family and brought this child as a gift to you. She is blessed with divine powers, and we have chosen your loving family to support her as she develops and grows," the angel shared. The heavenly messenger then held out the baby in her large hand to place into Julia's arms that were outstretched at the same time. Their eyes locked on the baby being delivered to their arms, and they began to gush over the little miracle.

"The hospitality I have experienced here today is no doubt a reflection of your lives together and those around you that you serve in your home and community everyday. This is a fine family to raise her as she takes on the tasks ahead of her," the guardian finished.

With the ending of her declaration, a quick gust of wind blew through the patio. After covering the baby, shielding her from the wind, the new parents looked back up to where the angel had stood, but she had vanished. Just a moment too late, Javier looked up to thank Angela, and she was nowhere to be seen. The couple quickly stood to head for the door back into the house in an attempt to search for Angela. There, standing in the doorway, was Maria in her robe and sandals looking confused.

"What's going on? I was closing my window and saw a bright light! Wind rushed through the house; I nearly fell out of my *huaraches*!" she demanded.

She suddenly noticed the baby in Julia's arms and tears in her eyes. Her eyes widened.

"Oh Mama, you won't believe what just happened," Javier responded emotionally.

Chapter 2
Rene

Divine powers? What could that possibly mean? They all thought that night as they explained to Maria what just happened there on the patio.

"Well, she's a gift from an angel," Javier assured his family aloud.

"And Divine is of God or goodness. So there's that," Julia expressed as she gazed down smiling with pride at the baby in her arms, caressing her cheek and adjusting the blanket to keep her warm.

"Well, until you figure it out, raising this baby in this public hotel may not have the privacy you might need, powers or no powers. You need time alone with her. Go to my father's house in Còrdoba. You know it hasn't been used in a while," Maria recommended.

"*Sí*, Mama. That is true. We will go right away, and I will return to settle things here in a couple of days," Javier immediately agreed.

"I know you're *Señor* 'World Traveler,' *Mijo*, with all your books and stories, but I'm YOUR mother still. I will take care of things here. Your brothers will help me, and God knows Tomàs needs to stop chasing different girls. He can do more," she said, shaking her head in disapproval. "Take all the time you need," she insisted.

The new parents then packed up their necessities and headed into the night for the *Casita Feliz*.

It was along the long ride to Còrdoba that the couple decided her name, or was it maybe they were *told* her name? The wagon ride was bumpy, and the little wren was there for the journey, tweeting away in the cage seated next to Julia.

"Oh now you're speaking, *Chica*?" Javier questioned the bird. "You were so quiet the whole ride to Mexico; now you have something to say?" Then looking over at his wife he added, "You think she knows the baby is here?" Javier asked Julia with a laugh.

"That's silly, Javi. But hey, after what happened tonight- why doubt anything," she joked back.

The little wren, still chirping loudly from under the cloth that covered its cage, was now a chatterbox. Julia became concerned for the bird since the baby was snoozing away, looking angelic. She peeked under the cloth to take a look at the wren when the bird then flew right at their side of the cage as if to get a closer look at the baby in her arms. It was odd she didn't fly away in fear as expected. Clinging to the bars of the cage with its little feet, its little eye was rapidly observing the baby with its head tilted as it stopped tweeting.

"*Chica* is studying the baby. Maybe she wanted to take a look at her new friend," Julia called out to Javier, who was focused on the dark road ahead. Javier just chuckled.

"What kind of bird was this again you said?" Julia said, slightly inspired.

"A wren," Javier reminded her.

"A wren," Julia softly repeated. "Wren… ay…" Julia mumbled in thought as names for the baby were tumbling through her head as the wagon wheels jumbled along the road.

"Who's Rene, *Amor*?" Javier questioned, immediately tilting his head back towards Julia to hear her better.

"I didn't say 'Rene,' Javi." she replied.

Just then the baby's eyes opened, and the bird began chirping again. This was the first time Julia had seen her daughter's eyes since her arrival. Tiny eyelashes had only been twitching about between her closed eyelids that night. They were hazel and just as bright as the Angel's that gifted her to them.

"Rene?" Julia repeated looking down at the little girl, dropping the cloth that covered the birdcage.

The baby's eyes met hers, and she smiled. Julia got chills down her spine, and the hairs on the back of her neck stood up underneath her thick hair. The baby girl then stretched out her arms over her head, yawned, and brought her hands together across her chest, smiling again.

"*Amor*! Who's Rene?" Javier asked again, looking back at his wife in the wagon. Julia looked at him in shock. Javier's head kept looking back and forth between her and the road ahead. He then stopped the carriage and waited for a response. "*Amor*?" He said again gently.

"Our daughter," Julia said as she looked up from the baby again. "I think her name is Rene."

"I had a cousin named Rene. He was a good man. But hey, I've heard of women with that name too at church," Javier assured his wife with a smile.

"It was like she heard her name and woke up." Julia said in disbelief, looking down at the baby.

Javier then gave it a try. "Rene? Is that you?"

Little Rene looked at her father and smiled.

Javier then reached down and caressed his daughter's face and greeted her, "Hello Rene. My little *Reina*." Rene then smiled and slowly blinked her eyes.

"I thought I was your *Reina*?" Julia teased, looking over at her husband.

"You are my queen, *Amor*! She's just a little one," Javier laughed as he turned back to get the horses started up again. "Hiya!" he hollered.

Just then the little bird covered in its cage started tweeting again.

"Okay! You're Reina too!" Javier called out to the bird.

"Oh, Javier. A true gentleman! But really, maybe *Chica* can be named Reina," Julia said.

"Okay! Now, what about a middle name? I mean if we don't have a son one day, can her middle name be Rolando? You know

23

I've wanted to name a son Rolando after my father, and, after all that's my middle name. A family name!" Javier rambled on as the carriage continued on their trek.

"Yes, Javi. She can be Rene Rolando Reyes." She said, smiling down at her daughter who had closed her eyes to go back to sleep as the wagon continued into the night.

Time quickly passed for the Reyes family in Córdoba, and just as quickly, Rene grew from infant to young child.

Rene shot up in her bed in the corner of the house with a scream that lit every candle in their bedroom ablaze. Her parents awoke and ran to her side in fear for their daughter's safety. It was a nightmare again.

Two and a half years had passed since Julia and Javier brought their daughter to Còrdoba one hundred miles east of Puebla to raise her in secret. The mention of "Divine Powers" that their new daughter would possess both troubled and intrigued their minds.

Rene was an amazing sleeper as an infant. In fact, sleeping was never a problem for her until recently. Maybe it was because she grew and matured twice as fast as a normal child had been known to grow. Accelerated growth was one of characteristics this divine being possessed. As many parents would attest to sleepless nights for their newborn and infants, that wasn't the case for Julia and Javier. Though they were conveniently located in a town where coffee was processed *en masse*, extra cups to energize them were never needed. But something was different now. This was the second time Rene had been jolted awake from a nightmare.

The town was peaceful, and their home was fairly secluded on the outskirts. The house only had two rooms; a bedroom in one, where the three of them slept, and the other was the common room with the kitchen and sitting area. The house had a large front patio, a small private courtyard protected by walls, a barn in the rear, and was surrounded by many trees.

Javier and Julia found parenting agreeable and easy to be around each other so much. Javier had stopped traveling overseas too when the baby came. The two took turns visiting Puebla to check on things back in town where Maria was successfully managing things as she promised she could. Javier's brothers would sometimes bring Maria to visit Rene in Còrdoba for holidays and at least once a month just for fun. Rene loved her visiting family just as much as her own parents. Everyone seemed happy and carefree, so what was going on to cause these nightmares?

The biggest concern the two did have for their daughter up to this point was mostly "*What is she gonna do next?!*" as Rene revealed her different gifts since they arrived at the old Feliz house. The first presented itself the moment they entered the dusty old abandoned like casita. Rene sneezed, and the old candles sitting in the house all lit up! The two looked at each other and down at Rene who was now awake taking it all in.

The second gift aside from her accelerated growth and learning abilities was she didn't mind heat. Meaning, when Rene was only '3 months old,' she weaseled out of her mom's arms to crawl across the patio floor on a hot afternoon. Not even thinking the floor would be hot, the parents just observed her crawling away into the sunlit part of the patio. Dazzled by the red hairs that highlighted her head like a crown, they watched her find a leaf nearby. Rene was happily sitting on the ground in her diaper and small shirt, legs out in front and hands to her sides supporting her off and on as she played.

Javier headed towards her after a minute barefooted. Upon reaching the sunlit part of the patio, he exclaimed, "Ouch! It's hot!"

Julia jumped up into her sandals and ran to the baby who was still laughing and smiling, as she appeared to be studying her leaf. Javier forgot about his burning feet as he picked up Rene, checking her hands and legs for burns or red marks.

"Is she ok?" Julia asked as she also inspected the baby in frantic concern.

"I guess so," Javier shrugged as he took her back into the shade. "My feet are probably blistered, but... she is perfect as usual," he said in awe.

"Okay, so our daughter seems to be fire resistant like the boys in the Bible? Wow," Julia said with sarcasm and confusion.

"Divine powers, Angela told us," Javier recalled as he exhaled in relief.

"What else can you do, *Mija*? You are full of surprises!" Julia questioned Rene, kissing her chubby cheek as Javier placed her in her mother's arms. Rene giggled. The parents wondered how this gift was going to support Rene's tasks ahead of her.

However, these nightmares were unsettling for the parents. What was going on in Rene's mind?

"Maybe it was something we read to her that is getting in her mind, disrupting her sleep? But what?" Javier asked, as Julia had picked up Rene to cry on her shoulder as she patted her back in an attempt to comfort her.

"A train," Rene cried as she copied her mom and began to pat her back in return. Rene, who was only delivered a little over 2 years ago, now had the appearance of a near 5 year old girl. Accelerated growth. Rene pulled away from her mom and continued, "A train fell into the river, and people died."

"Who told you that Rene?" Javier questioned, looking at Julia who shook her head in response with a shrug.

"In my dream. I saw it," Rene said sniffling sadly, looking down at her own hands almost in shame.

Her parents just looked at her in concern waiting for her to finish as her father moved the hair across her face behind her ear. Rene was very articulate, as she was also mature for her age. Her gift of accelerated learning, topped with the constant surrounding of only adults who visited her at home aided in that development, minus Tomás, who never seemed to grow up. He was Rene's best playtime partner when he came to town, a fun uncle who even played dolls with her.

"The train was on a bridge, and it broke. There was a fire." She said wringing her hands as if she was guilty. "Did I do that?" Rene asked quietly.

"*Mija*, no! No way! You were here in bed, and you've never been on a train," Julia assured her daughter.

"But," Rene continued. "But I…" she stuttered slightly.

"Rene, *mi amor*. Yes, you do light candles here at home but, you are strong," he reminded her as he gently tapped her forehead with his finger. "You can control it and get stronger everyday. This was a dream, and you had nothing to do with it, ok?" Javier explained. Rene nodded and began to relax slightly as her tears stopped.

"Ok, *Papi*," Rene replied in relief. "I just felt like I was there," she said, exhausted as she placed her head back on her mother's shoulder. Julia held her a moment and placed her back down in bed.

"Dreams are like that, *Niña*. They seem real; I know," she told Rene as she rubbed her back.

"Yes but, what do I say to that hurt man who was walking to me!?" She shot up again in bed to add, worried.

"Ask him if he needs help. Do not be afraid. It's your dream, and maybe he needs help," her father suggested. "We help people remember?" Javier finished as he stroked her cheek.

"Yeah. That's why we have Reina. You helped that lady, *Papi*." Rene said with a yawn laying back down.

"That's right," Julia added. "Don't be afraid. You are brave, Niña."

"Ok, Mama." Rene replied as she settled down at last and closed her eyes.

Julia and Javier kissed her head and headed back to bed, putting out the lit candles along the way. They laid down, wished each other good night, and sealed it with a kiss.

The couple woke up early the next morning and sat outside to enjoy some coffee, watching the sun rise through the trees, and listening to the birds playing. Reina was sitting in her cage on a nearby table and joined the birds in song.

Julia and Javier did this often in order to share quality time alone together at home. Javier loved coffee but Julia only drank it to commune with her husband before Rene woke up. The smell of coffee would always make Julia think of Javier when he was away on his trips, so having him home since the baby came was another great blessing.

"That dream must have really worn her out last night. She usually would be awake by now," Javier said as he leaned back in his chair to look into the open house door.

"I just hope she resolved her troubles. I hate getting nightmares myself. You're lucky you don't get any dreams too often," Julia commented with a shiver.

"True. I just wished I could sleep in general as well as you two do. When the sun is up, I am up," he added as he took a drink of coffee. "You make the best coffee, *Amor*. I will never make it come out like you do," he finished as he took his wife's hand and kissed it.

"Speaking of coffee. We need more. Can you get more when you take the horses out for a ride today please?" Julia requested.

"Your wish is my command, *Corazón*. I'll go now actually, I feel it's going to be hot again today," he replied, kissed her, and headed for the small barn. He mounted the black Andalusian and leashed the second, a young, brown-spotted horse to follow beside him.

Once across town, Javier laced the horses' leads to a post after a long trot and headed into a nearby market. As he kindly smiled and passed the merchant behind the counter, he noticed a newspaper article hanging behind her. "*Morelos Railway Accident. 200 people dead, 40 injured. Train plummets from unsupported bridge into San Antonio River.*" Dated June 24, 1881. Javier stopped in his tracks and leaned over the counter to read the article, his mouth opened in shock. The merchant stood nearby looking at him, slightly worried and irritated.

"*Señor*, that paper is old news. You didn't hear about it?" she inquired as she looked at him concernedly.

"I may have been traveling overseas at the time. No. I didn't hear of it." Javier quickly replied to the cashier, looked over at her, then down at the counter he was lying on to see the article. He quickly jumped off, his boots hitting the floor loudly, and stood as he adjusted his vest back into place trying to wipe the look of shock off his face.

"I'm sorry," he quickly apologized. "I didn't mean to jump on your counter. I don't get out of the house much to shop since my wife usually takes care of the shopping," he added in embarrassment. The merchant just shyly stared at Javier in a side glance, eyebrows raised for a minute wondering what he may do next.

"Can I just get a pound of coffee, *por favor*? Sorry for the trouble," Javier quickly asked, eyes anxiously shifting around the store. The girl turned her body to reach for the sack of beans behind her, nervously not taking her eyes off Javier.

"So you didn't lose a loved one in the wreck I'm guessing, since you didn't hear about it?" she asked.

"No. Right. I did not. Did you?" Javier replied, still anxious.

"Yes. He was my fiancé. We were to be married that August. He was a soldier," she recalled as she looked at the paper and back at Javier.

"I'm so sorry to hear that. Sorry for your loss," Javier uttered solemnly as he handed her the money for the coffee. He then noticed a butterfly on her necklace and added, "That's a beautiful necklace," trying to change the subject with an optimistic smile while putting away his money clip.

"Thank you," She said, "Juan gave it to me right after we met. He used to call me his butterfly. He was outgoing, and I'm the shy one," the girl responded as she gripped the charm on her necklace.

Javier kicked himself on the inside and muttered under his breath, *Ok, Big Mouth, let's go!* He thanked her for the coffee and apologized for any inconvenience he was causing and hurried out the door.

As Javier returned home, housed the horses, and fed them in the barn, he could hear Rene laughing with her mother in the yard. He smiled at the thought of her feeling better since the nightmare and headed into the courtyard.

"*Papi!*" Rene hollered as she ran with open arms into his. He bent over to hug her as he gently rocked her side to side in embrace.

"Good morning, *Mi Niña.*" Javier said lovingly. "You woke up late today!"

"I know," Rene confessed, "but I had to help that man!" she added with a tone of determination.

"The one in your dream? What did he say?" He asked anxiously, remembering the conversation in the store he just had.

"Juan said, *Tell my butterfly I love her and miss her, but she has to let me go now,*" Rene said in dictation, happily.

Javier's jaw dropped.

Unphased by her father's demeanor, Rene added, "*Papi!* I want a butterfly. I can never catch one. I will keep her forever!" Rene then looked up to the sky with her arms open to twirl.

Javier snapped out of it, shaking his head and responded, "Oh, is that right? I'll work on that ok? Let's go get Reina for now." He motioned towards the house. Julia, sensing something was wrong, mouthed "What happened?"

"I'll tell you later," he whispered as he handed her the bag of coffee.

Early the next day, Julia headed for the market before it opened, careful to not let anyone see or notice what she was up to. She pulled a note from her bag and quickly slid it under the door and hustled back home. It read:

My beautiful Mariposa,
Please stop hiding from your future.
I love you and miss you, but you have to let me go.
I want to see you happy again.
Love, Juju

"My daughter is full of surprises," she reminded herself quietly as arrived back home and opened the door. Javier and Rene looked up from their shared book on the table at Julia as she entered and smiled.

CHAPTER 3
Last Song

"Marisol has gone to Mexico City. She was ready to move on, she said. She even took down the newspaper we had here, she hid enough here in the store," the middle aged man at the counter replied to Julia, looking over her purchases.

Julia had gone to the market the following week to pick up a couple things and spoke to the man working there. Noticing the usual girl working was not there, she asked about her. Of course, she wanted to know what came of the letter she had delivered the week before, without revealing it was she who wrote it.

"Did you know Marisol, *Señora*?" the man continued.

"Oh, no, not very well, I just see her every time I come for groceries," Julia quickly answered.

"I'm happy my daughter has decided to move on, and my sister is happy to have her come and stay a while too. She is finally putting her past behind her," he finished, as he placed her goods in the sack she brought.

Julia nodded in agreement with a smile, paid the merchant for her groceries, and went home. Her mind wandered as she thought of her own parents and siblings also living in the big city. She had not seen them in a long time, she reminded herself.

Julia refocused on her walk home and hurried along, as Maria would be visiting soon along with Tomás.

"Mama Mia!" Rene hollered as her parents opened the door to welcome their mother and brother, throwing her arms around her grandma's hips for a hug. Rene had nicknamed her grandmother Mia since that's the best she could pronounce Maria at one point, and it stuck, but she also called her Nana.

"I missed you! I was crying for you, Mama Mia!" she added dramatically.

Maria looked down at her granddaughter who was indeed bigger than last she saw her and said, "*Aye, Mina*, I cried for you too! I couldn't wait to see you again." She patted her head and caressed her face as Rene looked up at her.

"Ok Rene. Let Nana come inside! She had a long ride here," Javier instructed with a chuckle as he guided his mother into the house. Rene took her hand in hers and dragged her in towards the kitchen area.

"Well, I did all the hard work, *hermano*!" Tomás remarked as he laid down their bags and shook his brother's hand, followed up with a hug.

"Listening to your complaints and not jumping off the wagon was harder work for me, *Hijo*," Maria quipped, giving Tomás a sideways glance and rolled her eyes before looking back at Rene.

"Uncle Tomás said he will be the baby, and you can be the mama when you play with dolls today, *Mija*," Maria whispered not so quietly to Rene with a chuckle. Rene giggled sweetly in return covering her mouth with her hand.

"Ok! I'll go get my toys!" Rene quickly added, leaving Maria in the kitchen with Julia as she ran into the bedroom. Even Reina sensed the excitement in the room and tweeted loudly in her cage nearby.

"Let me take those for you, Maria." Julia offered with open hands.

Maria removed her hat and cape and handed them to her daughter-in-law. "Thank you, yes, take these things away please. No more disguises needed here," She said with a smile.

"What is a disguise, Mama Mia?" Rene asked with curiosity as she re-entered the room with her arms full of dolls and toys. The house was small, but Rene's hearing was also sharp. Another gift.

"Things you cover yourself with so people don't see your wrinkles," Tomás snidely remarked under his breath with a cough. Javier quickly elbowed his brother in the ribs as Maria gave him an evil look.

"A disguise is something you wear so people won't know who you are, *Amor*." Julia answered, looking over at her inquisitive daughter.

"Ohhhh," Rene responded. She put her index finger on her chin and stared off for a second as she committed this information to memory.

"But why do you need it for?" She inquired again.

"I just do it to keep me safe, *Mija*. It covers my beauty when I travel to see you. People might think Uncle Tomás finally had a

36

wife to go out of town with, so I dress like an *hombre*," Maria answered. She then put on her head wrap from her bag, smiling at Rene before wiping it off to look at Tomás, who was rolling his eyes. Javier and Julia chuckled and shook their heads.

Later that night, everyone settled into their sleeping areas. Javier and Julia had gone to bed in their room, and Tomás wrapped himself in his poncho with a blanket holding his "bottle" in his hammock, while Maria and Rene lay awake. They were propped up against some pillows in their temporary bed made up in the common room, chatting away quietly. Rene loved when Nana spent the night. Having her close seemed to put her at ease more at bedtime. There were no nightmares when Nana came over.

Rene told her all about her nightmare she recently had. She told her how she also helped "Juan and his butterfly" and how she asked Papi for one too.

"*Mira, Niña,*" Maria quickly answered Rene. Maria reached into her nearby bag to grab some yarn and scissors. Rene observed the magic workings of her grandmother's hands. She quickly wrapped the yarn around her fingers on one hand, and after a few knots and bows and snips of the scissors, a butterfly was born.

"This one you can keep forever," Maria said as she held up the yarn butterfly hanging from another long piece of yarn from her hand.

"Wow, Nana! It's a miracle!" Rene beamed.

"No, *Mija*. You're a miracle. God has given you great gifts to help people," she remarked, giving Rene a big kiss on the cheek as she handed her the butterfly.

As Rene gently stroked the butterfly, she studied it. "I have something that can help you manage your nightmares too," Maria continued. Rene carefully put down the butterfly and held out her hands and closed her eyes tightly, waiting for another gift. Maria placed her hands under Rene's and folded them together between her own. Rene opened her eyes and curiously looked at her Nana.

"Rene, this is a gift of prayer. My father taught it to me when I was little like you. Long ago, my people prayed to the God of Wind," Maria shared. "Now we can pray to the God of everything! He loves and protects us all!" Rene's eyes widened in astonishment as she intently listened to her grandma. "Close your eyes and repeat what I say, Rene…"

Now I lay me down to sleep… I pray The Lord, "My soul to keep…" If I should die before I wake… I pray The

Lord, "My soul to take..." God bless my Mama and my Papa... My Nana's and my Tata... my Tia's and my Tio's... and everyone I should pray for... Please let me have good dreams... and make me a good girl... Amen.

As time went on, Rene practiced her prayer. She was able to manage her dreams even better. Not to say the occasional whimper, sob, or jolt of fear didn't set in, because they did; but the frantic awakenings with sudden candle lighting stopped. Julia and Javier were relieved, not that they feared the thought of the home catching fire since it was covered in clay. Worst case scenario, they would feel like they were in a large, heated oven. However, the thought of enjoying some one-on-one time as a couple was pressing on their thoughts since they shared a room with Rene and every waking hour with her as well.

"*Amor*, I was thinking of asking Mama to come stay with Rene for a few days. We can trade places in Puebla to celebrate our 8th anniversary at the hotel this December," Javier shared with his wife.

"Do you think Rene is ready for that? Do you think Maria can manage?" Julia questioned nervously without a pause for thought. "I mean, Rene is doing better, but you know me. I just worry at the beginning of a new idea," she finished with a nervous laugh.

Javier took Julia's small shoulders between his large hands and looked her in the eyes. He assured her that everything would be fine and reminded her this would be healthy for their relationship. Julia leaned into Javier for a hug and agreed.

Javier arranged for the occasion, and the plans were set. Everyone enjoyed their visits. Maria enjoyed having Rene to herself and taught her more about God, prayers, and art with yarn. Julia and Javier had a delightful weekend back home in Puebla. Of course, Julia would become tense and worried about her baby back in Cordóba, since she'd never left her before. Javier would be the reassuring voice of reason that Rene was in good hands with Maria. Remembering that Maria had been successfully overseeing both the hotel and gift store over the past three years, Rene would not be troublesome. She was still, despite managing the powers growing in her, the kind of baby that would make you want to have ten more if they would be that easy.

The thought of having even just one more child, if God were willing, was a desire the two would talk about on occasion. This weekend away was a time the two needed to take advantage of, being alone together back in their wing of the hotel. Javier even carried Julia over the threshold to their bedroom in remembrance of their wedding night.

Another year passed in Cordóba, and another anniversary was spent at their *posada* in Puebla. It was mid February, and Julia and Javier also noticed that their daughter's growth was surely slowing down a lot compared to the previous months and years. Checking their doorway markings where Rene stood every so often for growth updates confirmed their speculations.

"Am I bigger, *Papi*?" Rene asked. Her father removed the book from her head as she stood against the wall for a measurement marking.

"Just a little, *Niña*. Looks like you're going to stay my 'little' *Niña* a little longer," he answered as he squeezed her cheek and smiled. Rene looked up at her father, sensing there was more he wanted to share. Javier then continued as suspected. "You know, your mama and I have been talking about when we could move back to the *posada* with you, where we could be with Nana and closer to the others," Javier continued.

"Really? I hope soon!" Rene replied with excitement as a big smile covered her face.

"Soon enough, *Amor*." Javier assured her, smiling back. Rene nodded at her father in anticipation and headed out to the courtyard where Reina was singing. Just then, Julia rushed up to Javier with a notebook in hand.

"Javi!" She gasped with excitement. "Looks like we got an anniversary present this year!" She showed Javier the side notes she kept in her diary. Javier quickly leaned in and studied her book as he took it from her hands.

"Can it be?!" His eyes widened with excitement as he looked up at his wife, who had moved her hands up to mouth to cover her quivering lips, her eyes welling up with tears. She nodded in confirmation. Javier dropped the diary and his measurement book to the floor and joyfully hugged his wife tight.

"God is good," he whispered as he embraced his wife.

Julia just nodded, and after a moment had passed, she pleaded, "Okay, *Amor*. Let's not squeeze him out just yet! Your arms are so powerful like a vice."

Javier let her go, looked down at his wife, traced her face with his hand, and leaned down to kiss her sweetly. His eyes then continued down to her stomach, and he proceeded to caress it carefully.

As time continued, Julia's belly grew with the pregnancy. Now surpassing the time they lost the last baby, and the point came where the bump wasn't as un-noticeable. By now, Rene, who had the more mature look of an almost 9 year old after only 4 years past arrival, had the education and maturity of a young teenager. Though she still had much of her childlike innocence her parents did well to preserve, she was beginning to notice her mother looked different. One day in early May, she decided to inquire about her changing appearance as they sat outside together.

"Mama, your *pansa* looks like you're eating more tortillas than me or something," she joked carefully and curiously.

Julia, who had been looking over at Reina with concern sitting on a nearby table in her cage, now looked over at her daughter. She brought her hands up to her stomach as if to hold the growing baby inside. "Yes, Rene. My stomach is growing, but it's more than just tortillas in there," Julia chuckled. She looked down at her stomach and back at her daughter who was looking at her, still waiting for an answer.

"It's a—" Julia started to say, but Rene interrupted.

"Baby?" Rene finished her mothers sentence.

"How did you know?" Julia asked, looking at her slightly shocked.

"I had a dream. I was holding my doll, and when I looked down at it, it was a boy not a girl anymore, and he was crying. Then I saw you and Papi standing there looking down at us," Rene shared. Javier, who had been inside reading but overheard the conversation the girls were having, now joined them outside.

"Of course you would dream that," he scoffed, eyes and hands raised up to the sky with a defeated eye roll. However, he quickly looked down and smiled at Rene.

"I just didn't know it meant something. Everyone was happy, except this crying baby I held. So I didn't dwell on it much," she added, looking down at her empty arms as she described the dream. "When will he be here?"

"We're thinking by the beginning of September, but we didn't know he was a HE," Julia noted looking at Rene, head tilted with curiosity, waiting for her to answer.

"Well, the baby in my dream looked a little like Uncle Tomás," she said with a laugh. "But of course, much smaller. He stopped crying when I started to rock and bounce him a little. His eyes were brown like yours and Papi's, not mine. One looked different than the other though," she said with a tone of confusion as she looked up at her parents.

Julia looked up concernedly at Javier who was standing beside where she sat, grabbing his hand tightly that was on her shoulder. She looked back at Rene, as did Javier who patted her hand in reassurance.

Rene quickly apologized, sensing the uneasy demeanor in her mother, "I'm sorry. Maybe I shared too much?"

"No, *Mija*." Javier quickly interjected, as he quickly moved in front of Rene getting down on his knee. "Never stop sharing with us. We want to hear all your stories, dreams, ideas, and questions. You have many gifts, and you are a gift to us all," he finished as he took her hands in his and patted them to comfort her.

Rene smiled at her father but deep down still felt a sort of guilt for what she shared, mostly with her mother who looked so concerned for the new news. It seemed she was worried about something she shared. Maybe she'd be more careful around her mother with her words, she told herself.

As with new beginnings, death would also be part of life. It was only a month later that loss would be a part of Rene's personal life experiences.

Javier arose from bed early that one summer morning, as he usually rose with the sun. He quietly exited the room, closing the door behind him as he entered the common room. There was a strange silence that was not the norm as he approached Reina's cage in the kitchen area. Sitting on the countertop, the cage was covered with a cloth as usual for bedtime. Reina was usually chirping along with the birds outside who were waking up with the sunrise too. Javier slowly raised the cover off of the cage as he peered inside.

Reina was there sitting at the bottom of the cage with labored breathing, eyes slowly opening and closing. It was only a week ago that Rene had shared a dream with her father that Reina, her best friend at home, had flown away. The dream left Rene concerned for the little wren ever since. Everyone had noticed that as Rene had slowed her accelerated growth, Reina was also "slowing down." Rene knew that death was a part of life since she heard so many stories of her '*Tata Grande*' Rolando, who died when her father was only 15. Accepting that Reina was going to leave one day was something she couldn't do. The latest dream didn't help.

Javier then reached into the cage to hold the little wren, who continued her same posture of pain and weakness.

"*Pobrecita*," he whispered, looking at Reina with sadness.

Just then, the bedroom door opened, and the girls rushed toward him. Rene reached out her hands to take Reina from her father, and he placed her in her hands.

'I'm here, Reina. I'm here," she softly spoke to her little bird friend, gently stroking her feathers with her thumb.

As Rene walked away from her parents towards the back door, she continued, "If you need to go, you can go." Her voice shaking, she continued, "I will tell my brother all about you one day. Thank you for your songs, and thank you for being my friend."

As she stepped out the back door, a gust of wind blew by, and Reina closed her eyes for the last time. It was as if the wind had come down to take her spirit away at that exact moment. Julia and Javier stood behind Rene as her tears began to flow, and her shoulders shook from the sobs that left her mouth.

Javier pulled a handkerchief from his pocket and placed it over Reina and scooped up the lifeless wren from his daughter's hands. Rene turned to embrace her mother as she continued to cry. After finding a small basket nearby his daughter undoubtedly weaved herself, he placed Reina inside wrapped in the handkerchief.

Reina was buried in her basket later that morning near the large tree where a swing hung for Rene. A tiny cross was fashioned from sticks and string and placed at the site, and the three of them took turns saying their final goodbyes. When Julia's turn to speak came up, she unfolded a piece of paper she had written on. Writing always helped her better communicate when she needed it most.

"Reina, you were a beautiful bird from the moment I met you. The sun lit up your brown feathers to reveal bright specks of red color, just like my Rene's hair. Javier told me a wren was a symbol of rebirth, and that gave me hope for better things to come. You even helped me to name my baby girl, who arrived just after you did. One of the happiest days of my life, and you were a part of it. Thank you for making us smile with happy songs and dances around in your cage. We will never forget you, *Niña*."

The following day, as the family sat outside looking up at the leaves dancing in the trees as the wind blew warm summer air through the courtyard, Rene broke the silence.

"Mama. Yesterday you said Reina and I arrived the same day. What did that mean?" She looked in her mothers direction, and Javier looked up from his book to face his daughter's inquiry as well. Julia took a deep breath and looked at Rene.

"You did not grow in my stomach like this baby here and the babies in the books we've taught you about," she admitted as she scooted closer to Rene. "*Mija*, when we tell you that you are a gift from God, we mean it. All babies are a gift from God, and you really were a GIFT from God."

"That's right," Javier added. "Like Reina was a gift from that woman I helped in Italy. An angel in disguise, that your Mama helped that day, gave us you."

Rene looked at her parents knowing that this was the truth. She had known she looked a little different from her family. Her hazel eyes, no one else had. Red highlights in her hair that shone in the sun her family would comment on when she played outside, also, no one else had. Having powers, lighting candles with her mind, and the dreams… the proof was all there and made sense.

"What did she look like?" Rene finally asked after a few moments of silence as she reflected on the facts. Rene seemed to take the news with ease. A sense of peace was upon her, calming her emotions, as another gift began maturing inside her.

"Come with me," Julia instructed. Javier helped Julia up off the blanket, and she waddled just enough to notice as she headed into the house followed by Rene and Javier.

As she entered the house, she made her way with purpose towards the corner of the kitchen area. She carefully shook free a wooden piece of molding that revealed a secret hiding place. The slot was just big enough to conceal a stretched canvas or two. Julia then reached in and slid one out. She nodded with a smile in remembrance and turned it to face Rene. Rene approached her mother and took the canvas into her hands and studied the artwork her mother had made.

It was a beautiful angel with enormous wings in pearl white. She had long braided hair that flowed down her chest, brown and red in color, and donned a beautiful, flowing, brown robe. She looked strong and sturdy, and, there, in her arms was a baby clothed in white.

"This is me too?" Rene inquired softly, eyes still locked on the painting.

"Yes, Rene. Your mother painted this the morning after we arrived here in Cordóba. Neither of us slept that night. We were just so excited to have you in our lives. Mama just had to capture the moment we first saw you in Angela's arms," Javier answered.

Julia removed another item from the slot and handed it to Rene; a small white blanket with gold trim that glistened in the window light, matching the one in the painting.

"And this was mine," Rene added, as if she knew this part.

"That's right, *Amor*." Julia said with a smile.

"If it weren't for your arrival, we would still be waiting to raise a child," Javier noted as he approached his daughter, placing his hand on her shoulder.

"Thank you for sharing this story with me." Rene replied graciously, gazing up at her parents. "Can we put this up in the house now? We shouldn't hide our pasts. Mama, it's a beautiful painting."

Julia nodded and kissed Rene on the head as she took the painting and set off to fulfill her daughter's request. After all, their visitors all knew the story. It was no secret to hide, at least on Javier's side of the family.

Chapter 4
Ana

September 8, 1893

Ding. Ding. The shop bell rang as a customer entered the store one warm afternoon in September.

"Hola, Isabel! How are you?" A very pregnant Julia greeted an old familiar face from behind the counter as a woman entered the door. After arriving back in Puebla a few weeks earlier, Julia was back at work, eager to see her old friends and customers, many still returning loyaly.

"Julia! You're back!" Isabel replied with excitement. "I'm well, how are you?"

Julia then came around the counter holding her belly as she waddled to face her friend.

"Pregnant!? Congratulations!" Isabel exclaimed. Julia glowed with pride. At last, pregnancy had agreed with her beautifully, even though she was anxious to meet the little miracle growing inside her. Julia then turned and reached back around the counter to guide Rene around the counter to meet the faithful customer.

"Very!" Julia confirmed with a big exhale and a smile. "Isabel, this is my daughter as well." Rene smiled and shyly waved at Isabel, staying at her mother's side.

"Wow. Julia! You have been busy while you were gone! As I expected anyway. You've always been a hard worker," Isabel stated. "What is your name, *Niña*?" She asked, turning to Rene.

"Rene," she shared. "But my friends call me Ren. At least they will when I get some friends," Rene added with a confident smile.

Isabel laughed, "Oh yes, Rene! They certainly will. You will have some in no time."

Rene smiled brightly and nodded in agreement. She was excited to be in Puebla with her family at last. She was also very excited and optimistic about meeting some friends her age too.

As Julia and Isabel conversed near the counter, Rene made her way to the front of the store to observe the plaza coming to life outside the window. She was enjoying people watching, when suddenly a little girl ran by the window and tripped on the sidewalk in front of the store. Rene quickly ran outside to check on her.

"Are you ok?" Rene asked concernedly, as she knelt down next to the fair, curly short-haired girl who was looking down at her scraped knee as she cradled her bent leg to get a closer look.

"Yea. It's not too bad. Mama will fix it for me later," she quickly answered as she looked up wincing in pain but stopped her hissing to ask, "What's your name?" The girl became quickly distracted by Rene's long braided hair coming down from her head.

"I'm Rene. This is my mama's shop here," she shared, pointing at the building beside them. The green in her hazel eyes became more dominant as she remained focused on the girl. Anticipation built. *Is this the friend I was going to meet?* Rene thought to herself.

"Rene? I'm Ana. Can I just call you Ren for short? I like short names," Ana quickly rambled as she picked herself up from the floor, straightening out her dress and fixing her sandals. She noticed Rene was bare footed. *Surely bare feet don't trip*, Ana thought to herself.

"Sure!" Rene exclaimed. "Hi, Ana."

Just then, Julia walked out the shop door making the bell ring, getting the girls' attention. Isabel followed behind her, also exiting the store.

"Everything ok out here?" Julia questioned concernedly.

"I'll see you next time, Julia," Isabel quickly whispered loudly as she pat Julia's arm and headed off into the Plaza.

Julia nodded and waved over her shoulder at Isabel as she stayed focused on the girls.

"Yes, Mama. This is Ana. I saw her fall, so I came to ask if she was ok." Rene explained, motioning at the shorter girl standing next to her.

Julia quickly scanned Ana and noticed her scraped knee. "Oh Ana, your knee. Are you ok?" she quickly inquired with care, still holding her shop door open.

"Ya. I'm ok. It's not bad. My Mama is a doctor. She can fix it later," Ana replied with certainty.

"Oh good! Yes. I'm sure she will. That is a great mama to have," Julia replied with a smile.

"I guess." Ana shrugged as she quickly looked back at Rene. "Well, I better go. My sister won't wait long for me. She hates waiting, but she has to because mama said it is not safe to be alone."

"That is good advice, Ana." Julia agreed, looking at Rene in hopes that she caught the lesson in the message.

"Where are you going?" Rene immediately asked with a hint of anxiety. She didn't want her new friend to leave so soon.

"Over to the river. We play there when it is hot enough," Ana replied, as she motioned up to the bright sunlit sky. "Wanna come?" Ana offered. Just then another girl's voice called from a distance "Ana! Hurry up!" Ana quickly turned to the direction of the voice and hollered back, "Ok! I'm coming!"

Rene looked up at her mom, her anxiety and excitement built up inside her, eyes growing wider and greener. It was as if she were trying to influence her mother's mind with her own. Julia was startled by her daughters changing eyes for a moment.

"Ok. But, just for a little bit," Julia replied with a hint of reluctance from worry, but somehow she felt deep down like she could trust her. Rene then hugged her mother tightly around the waist, smiling from ear to ear.

"Thank you, Mama!" she exclaimed, and her eyes faded back to the more common hazel mixed colors of brown and green as Ana, then ran off.

"Oh! *De nada*, Rene! Okay. Go!" Julia grunted as she patted her daughter's back with her one free hand. Rene released her mother and bolted off towards Ana and her sister in the distance.

Julia let out a big exhale thinking, *She feels almost as strong as Javier*. As she caught her breath, she began to experience pain on the side of her stomach. She pressed her palm into her side in hopes to relieve the pain and took deep breaths. She waddled back into the shop as she continued to feel out of breath, alongside the growing pain.

Rene easily caught up with Ana just as Ana had reached her sister. She was another fair skinned girl with longer, bushy hair. Rene caught her breath quickly. The gift of athleticism was growing inside her more strongly now. As the other girls still struggled to catch theirs, they all looked down the rock slope that led to the narrow part of the river below, thinking of where to start their descent.

"This is Ren," Ana motioned at Rene, pointing her thumb at her. Her careless introduction to her older sister was short lived as they continued to take heavy breaths.

"Oh," The older girl replied in between breaths, still looking down at the river, mentally mapping a way down the slope to get near the water. She didn't seem as friendly or talkative as Ana.

The three girls carefully made their way down to the water, where the two sisters removed their sandals. "This is Lidi. That's short for Lidia. She's my old sister," Ana motioned nonchalantly towards her sister while looking at Rene.

"Ana, I'm only two years older than you. I'm not an old lady," Lidi quickly barked back.

"Okay. 'Older.'" Ana replied mockingly, rolling her eyes.

"Hi Lidi," Rene said with a smile, looking at Lidi who was pushing her bounty of hair behind her ears, slightly annoyed looking, most likely from her sister's snide remark.

"*Ciao*," Lidi irritatedly replied.

"That means *Hi* or *see you later* in Italian." Ana quickly explained, as a confused look crossed Rene's face. "We're half Puerto Rican and half Italian. We just moved here from New York a couple months ago."

"I see," Rene replied. As confusion turned to curiosity on Rene's face, she quickly thought to herself, *I need to learn Italian.*

"Some people don't like that around here," Ana shared, as she looked down in shame for a moment and back at Rene for her reaction.

Rene shrugged. "I don't mind. You're nice to me," she acknowledged with a smile, but also wondered what she meant by the '*some people don't like that around here*' remark.

Ana smiled, going back to the event at hand.

"We didn't have nice rivers like this in New York with all the big buildings and streets. I mean there's the ocean but *eh*. So we love coming here to play," she went on to share.

"Me too. Well, my family just moved back here too, but there was one by my old house. I feel like the river is talking when the water rolls over the rocks," Rene explained, looking back at the river, scanning over the waters with her eyes, motioning with her hand, wiggling her fingers in little wavy motions. Ana liked the way Rene described the river like that.

"Well, it's not too deep here, but it is further down," Ana remarked. "I don't like the darker parts, like the ocean," she finished with a shiver of fear.

Rene quickly waded into the river. Her legs felt powerful even with the current pushing her along. She pushed herself forward into the deeper water and started to swim around looking back at Ana. She was fearless in the river, and Ana admired Rene's courage. Inspired, she waded in the water but just went in enough to sit where the water was deep enough to touch her neck. Ana laughed as Rene splashed and moved around the water like an otter, while Lidi sat nearby at the water's edge. She was less interested in going into the river. Her pants were rolled up high enough to let her feet rest in the water as she picked flowers growing nearby her.

After an hour, Rene reminded them that she couldn't stay long, and the girls headed back to town. The gift shop was the first stop back into the plaza.

"Can we visit again tomorrow?" Rene asked Ana when she stopped at the shop door.

"Sure! We'll come by again tomorrow to get you. Hopefully, I don't trip again!" Ana laughed.

"Okay! See you tomorrow. Be careful!" Rene chuckled back, waving and grabbing the shop door with the other hand. As Ana and her sister walked away towards the plaza, Rene happily swung open the shop door. The bell clanged loudly, matching Rene's energy level.

"Rene, is that you?" Julia suddenly called out, but was nowhere to be seen.

"Mama? Where are you?" Rene responded, slightly concerned by the tone in her mother's voice.

She waited for an answer as she started to hear heavy breathing and grunting. *Is that her?* She thought to herself; now growing uneasy in her stomach, she ran for the counter. As she rounded the corner, she quickly stopped and saw her mom sitting on the floor slumped against the wall, holding her stomach wincing in pain off and on.

"I think the baby is coming now, Rene. Go get your Papa!" Julia quickly responded to her daughter's worried look, catching her breath a moment. Rene nodded in response, as her eyes grew wide and lit green again. She bolted back out of the shop.

Ana was still nearby and noticed Rene coming out of the store. Curious as to why her friend was running like the wind, she shouted "Ren? Where you going?"

"Mama is having her baby! I'm getting *Papi*!" She called back with a quick glance at Ana as she continued to run off towards the *posada*.
"I'll get my Mama!" Ana called back and ran off towards her mother's clinic.

"You did so good, *Amor*." Javier praised his wife as he gave her a kiss on the head and caressed his son's face. "Thank you so much for being here, Dr. Rameriz. You are a skilled woman. A true blessing," he went on to tell Ana's mother, who was also kneeling near his wife on the floor, cleaning up her hands with a towel from her bag.

Doctor Rameriz humbly smiled and nodded. "*Señor*, It is my pleasure. I'm only a few doors away, so it was no trouble. The girls were quick thinkers today it seemed," She replied curiously, looking around for their daughters in the shop a second but quickly refocusing on Julia.

"Congratulations, *Señora*. Enjoy your new baby boy. He seems to be getting along well here." She glanced down at the baby at Julia's breast, who latched on quickly after birth, suckling on his mother. It was like he had not eaten in weeks. "You would do well to go home and rest now, *Señora*." the doctor sternly added as she stood with her bag. "Please come see me in a few days at my clinic, and we can have a little follow up exam for you both."

Javier arose with the doctor to shake her hand and thank her again.

"Please, Doctor. Call me Julia. I've been honored to have you here with me. Thank you so much for your help," Julia finally spoke, looking up at the doctor, breaking her stare from her cuddly little baby boy. She continued to pat his bottom while he nursed.

Dr. Rameriz smiled and nodded at Julia. She glanced at Javier who gently bowed at her in gratitude again. She smiled and bowed back. Once she passed the counter, she noticed Ana sitting on the floor with Rene on the other side. She silently motioned at Ana as she passed the counter, and the two left the shop.

"Rene. Come here, *Cariño*. Come see your little brother," Julia called out to her daughter as she ended her son's feeding.

Rene slowly arose from where she was sitting with Ana by the counter during her brother's screaming debut and made her way around the counter. Javier reached out to guide her with assurance to her mother's side.

"Thank you, Rene, for getting the doctor and your father. You were a great help to me too, *Amor*." Julia told Rene, as she knelt beside her looking down at the baby. She grabbed her daughter's head and pulled it towards her to eagerly kiss it. Rene peered down at the baby in her mother's arms.

"Here, hold him, Rene," Her mother instructed, as she leaned over to give the baby to the new big sister. Rene adjusted herself to sit on the floor firmly and put out her arms to receive the baby.

Wow. Much heavier than my dolls, Rene thought to herself as she studied the little boy in her arms. *He's got a round head and ears, like a teddy bear and Uncle Tomás,* she mentally noted with a smile. She looked at his hands and feet, as if to count to make sure they were all there as the baby slept peacefully. He was wrapped in the *sarape* she gave her parents over the counter during the final moments of labor before he was born.

"We are proud of you, Rene, You stayed calm and focused and did a great job getting everyone here for Mama," Javier finally said. His eyes were still a little watery from the roller coaster of emotions that just swept through the now closed up shop. He looked at his family in front of him and smiled in pride and continued, "This shop truly holds the treasures I most adore now."

The next day, Rene went to the shop with Maria, as her parents stayed behind with the new baby. Rene had begged to go back to the plaza to see her friend since before the baby excitement, they made plans to see each other together today. Maria agreed to take her and finish cleaning up the shop. She would take care of a few things while she was there, along with making a gift basket to thank the doctor again for her help.

Just as the two finished putting a few more gifts into the large basket the door opened, and the bell rang excitedly.

"What's his name?" Ana exclaimed as she ran to the counter, almost imitating a bull.

"Cristiano Javier Reyes," Rene answered with a smile. *Thank God, she remembered to come today,* she thought to herself.

"Oh, Cris! That's a nice name, like my little sister. She's Cristiana, T.T. for short," Ana shared, as her face turned from excitement to a look of annoyance thinking of her little sister. "She's so loud though, she's just a baby too."

"That's my mama's middle name too." She added as she laughed shyly.

"Well hopefully she grows up and is nice like your mama. Well, when she's not having a baby!" Ana laughed with great animation. Rene giggled along, covering her mouth.

"Okay girls, here is the basket for the good doctor. Go and take it to her now and be back in an hour please." Maria instructed, anxious to get the excitement level in the shop back down to normal. A hint of concern grew inside Maria about this new friend knocking something over. Her big energy and animation reminded her of her own four boisterous sons in their youthful years.

Rene and Ana held the large basket by the handles on each end, carrying it out of the shop as Ana complained about it being as heavy as her dogs. Nana even added a pineapple to it that she had bought from a nearby vendor that morning on the way to the shop. Pineapples were their family's favorite fruit. As the girls walked down the street to the clinic, Ana tripped again on her sandal but quickly caught herself from falling this time.

"*Goffa*. I know," Ana admitted. She went on to explain how that meant 'clumsy' in Italian, how she gets Lidi's hand-me-downs, and that her sister's big "clown feet" make her parents always buy her new shoes.

"I tried wearing no shoes like you, but my feet were burning yesterday!" Ana finished sharing as a sense of concern set in, worried she made fun of Rene for being shoeless. "Sorry, I didn't mean to say something about your feet," she quickly added.

"It's okay," Rene smiled. "I don't like sandals or shoes on my feet really. I just like to have bare feet, because my feet grew fast too and shoes didn't fit right all of the time," she concluded with a smile, ignoring to touch on the fact that hot floors didn't seem to bother her feet. Ana just nodded and smiled.

"Here's my mama's office," Ana motioned, sticking out her chin as she lugged the basket around Rene who had reached to open the door with one hand. "Geez, you're strong, Ren. This thing has a grocery store in it!" Rene just laughed at the humorous remark.

Maybe I am getting strong, Rene thought to herself curiously.

After dropping off the basket and heading out into the plaza, the girls noticed some kids playing kickball. Lidi was on a nearby bench with another older looking girl looking on at the game happening too. Ana and Rene decided to go over and get in on the fun.

After brief instruction by one of the kids who agreed to let the girls play, Rene took to the sport like a natural. She immediately gained points for her team, and the kids were excited. Well, at least half of them were, anyway. Rene played well with her team, and she dominated the game. Ana was half cheering and half trying to play the game, being uncoordinated as she already established over the past 24 hours. The final winning point was assisted by Rene, who stayed humble throughout the game. When Ana ran up to her to congratulate her friend, facing Rene for a hug, another girl ran up behind Rene and pushed her to the ground. Rene landed hard on her hands she had put out in front of her to break her fall, scraping her left knee on the stone floor along the way, causing it to bleed.

"Look at her! She doesn't even own shoes! *Pobre*! Look at that old dress and messy hair!" The bully went on to say, insulting Rene who was being helped up by Ana.

The Reyes family was by no means "poor," but showing off their wealth was never something they went about doing. Generosity, yes. Kindness, yes. Flashy clothes? Never. Besides, Rene had grown so quickly, wearing clothes that didn't fit perfectly was the usual for her. No one seemed to mind in her family, but this reality was different, as she slowly found out.

Ana immediately saw her friend's bloody knee and rushed up to the bully with all the courage she could muster and slapped the girl with all the strength she had.

"*Vacca!*" Ana screamed at the girl who was now clutching her face in shock.

Lidi quickly ran over to her sister's side and grabbed her arm, afraid she may strike again. Rene stood up and dusted off her hands, ignoring the scratch on her knee. She turned to face her assailant as she rushed in front of Ana and Lidi. As the bully continued to clutch her face out of embarrassment and pain, she shuddered as she caught a glimpse of Rene, who was giving a cold stare at her and the rest of the kids near her, breathing slowly. Her green eyes were lit green again, and a sense of intimidation fell over the crowd. They stepped back and looked at each other in confusion and worry, glancing nervously at Rene. Rene held her position a moment, looking over the crowd before turning back to Ana and Lidi.

"I'm ok. Let's go," Rene muttered, as she motioned her hand for them to follow her.

As the girls turned to leave, the crowd disbanded. The bully walked alone off into another area of the plaza, still holding her face as a few tears escaped her eyes and rolled down her cheeks. Ana took a minute to come around from her anger when Rene finally broke the silence.

"What did you call her? Cow?" Rene asked with uncertainty.

"Yeah," Ana suddenly laughed, smiling at Rene. "That's the same in Spanish and Italian." Rene laughed along for a second but quickly stopped. She felt a sort of guilt inside her for the bully being hit, who ended up walking away alone and crying.

Why did she push me? What made her mad? How sad no one checked up on her when Ana slapped her. These thoughts raced through Rene's mind.

    As Rene neared her family's shop the girls parted ways and said goodbye. Rene spotted Maria exiting the store and locking the door ahead of her and hurried over to her grandmother as she shook off her questions building up inside her.

"I saw you coming, *Niña*. We're going home. The shop can close early today," Nana told her when she caught up to her, as Maria turned and motioned for Rene to follow her. Rene nodded and remained quiet, concerned that maybe Nana had seen her coming and noticed her cut knee or knew what had happened in the plaza. As they headed out of the busy area of town, Maria spoke up.

"Did you have fun with your friend today?" Maria asked.

Maybe she didn't see anything! Rene thought to herself, feeling a little relieved.

"Oh, yes, Nana. Thank you for bringing me to the shop today," Rene quickly replied, trying to hide the worry in her voice as she smiled over at her Nana. They were almost the same height.

"Good, *Niña*. I'm glad." Maria replied with a smile, as she shifted her eyes down to see Rene's now red knee. The bleeding had stopped, and blood began to disappear. She had kept the discovery to herself thinking, *If Rene wants to share with me, she will.*

As the two of them continued to walk the mile back to the Posada and shared in general conversation along the way, Rene's mind continued to flood with thoughts.

Why was that girl mean? What did I do? Could I have stopped her? Why did Ana hit her?

As they arrived and entered the door, Rene spotted her father in the hall walking with her baby brother in his arms.

I'll ask Dad. He'll know. She told herself, immediately feeling better with the thought of his wisdom.

Javier immediately noticed his daughter and mother enter the door, looking up from the content baby in his arms. Maria smiled and waved at Javier before making her way towards the kitchen, but Rene, on the other hand, had an unfamiliar look on her face. His brow raised as he slowly made his way over to her, wondering what happened on her outing. He looked over his daughter and noticed some dirt at the edge of her dress. As he continued to observe her as she walked towards him, he noticed some redness on her knee. As she got closer to him, the redness disappeared and a tiny scar was left.

Rene had lived a more delicate life with her family up to this point, and encountering children her age seemed to be changing her suddenly. Perhaps they were awakening the powers still sleeping inside her that were never "needed" before now.

"*Papi*. I need to ask you something about today," Rene demanded respectfully.

"Yes, *Amor*? What is it?" Javier slowly replied, hiding his shock that his daughter seemed to heal before his eyes. "Wait. Let's go outside to get Cristiano some sun. Your Mama is taking a nap," he quickly added, motioning towards the patio door with his free hand and letting Rene lead the way.

CHAPTER 5
Downriver

Summer 1898

"So, that was some dream last night, huh Ren?" Ana joked to her friend as they swam in the river that was near her home one hot day. Rene was looking down at the riverbed beneath her, letting her feet slide over the smooth, water beaten-rocks in between paddles. Hearing this remark stopped her in her tracks; her eyes widened, and face went as white as a ghost's. She slowly looked up to face her friend, uncertain of what happened last night.

"Ummm…" Rene started to say before Ana cut her off.

"Hey, I'm not mad. I mean my boob just finally stopped hurting but it's fine. Lidi always hits me. Not when she's sleeping, but I'm tough," Ana chuckled trying to make light of the situation her friend seemed so obviously embarrassed about.

"I hit you!?" Rene exclaimed in horror. "Your boob!?" Rene gave her forehead a smack with the palm of her hand letting it slide down back into the water. She was mortified. *My dreams are back!* Rene told herself. She wanted to cry.

"It was probably just a nightmare, Ren. It's okay. I'm not mad. I mean you were kinda scary, but, you just sat up in bed on your knees, turned and looked at me with your eyes closed and BAM! You socked me right in the boob. I did hit you back, and you fell over and went back to normal sleep. Sorry I hit you back," Ana laughed. She did her best to not get mad at her friend. Rene had never hurt her before, and now she was usually the one protecting her once she learned some self-defense from her father. She knew how nightmares could be because sometimes Cristiana sleep walked around their little house. She could see that Rene was disappointed in herself, but didn't know ALL the reasons why.

It was just a punch in the chest. I'm over it. Ana thought to herself.

The past 4 years flew by for the girls. They were as close as sisters, maybe even closer than her sisters in Ana's case, and Rene only had her brother. Rene and Ana spent a lot of time together when they weren't doing home studies, church, family events, or helping out at their parent's businesses. They would find any reason to make their parents agree to an overnighter or daytime adventure together. Rene and Ana would pretend they were professional maids at times at the *posada* and help clean the rooms when guests left. They washed dishes and bedding and helped with Christiano; Julia always appreciated that. Ana loved it at Rene's house. Their whole family cooked and ate together for dinner. Plus, being at the "big house" reminded Ana of her old house in New York, and Rene had her own room like she used to have. But Rene loved it at Ana's house too. She appreciated their small home the most, because it reminded her of being back at the house in Còrdoba. Ana's house was also closer to the river, and Rene always felt peaceful and refreshed just being near the water. Ana also had pets, mostly dogs but also a donkey that was gifted to her mother by a patient in town. In a way, they reminded Rene of her first pet and friend in life, Reina, who was never far from her thoughts. Hearing birds sing and see them swoop down from the trees or bouncing along the tree branches near the river were everyday reminders. She would often dream of Reina too, sometimes causing her to wake up with some tears.

Dr. Rameriz and Julia also became friends as well, but for a different cause. As Rene's dream hinted before Cristiano was born, there was something different with one of his eyes. As he grew out of his infant stage and his eye color would become permanent, Julia had noticed a sort of cloudiness in the left eye. Concerned, she took him to Dr. Rameriz who confirmed that her suspicion was now fact. She had become his regular physician since his birth at the shop and found what appeared to be a tumor in the retina and noted he may have been blind since birth. She recommended that the family travel overseas to see a specialist, and, at 18 months old, little Cristiano underwent surgery to remove his eye. This was the best option to prevent the possible spread of the cancer to the other eye and cause total blindness or worse, even with the low survival rate. This challenge the family faced together seemed to take its toll the most on Julia. She was the natural worrywart, and Javier remained her steady emotional support as he always had.

Rene had concern for her brother as well but she was somehow optimistic, so the stress of the family's challenge didn't weigh on her too heavily. She knew her brother, who was already as wild as an animal for a post-toddler, would be strong and live through anything. Cris got up and ran at 9 months old and started climbing things like his sister not long after. Getting himself knocked around never seemed to faze him or halt his curiosity for long. Maybe he had his very own angel always looking out for him, aside from his big sister.

He too was intelligent. Cris loved puzzles and taking things apart to see how they worked, and he was also very athletic like Rene.

Even though he had sight in only one eye, his parents never told him there was something he could not do. Of course, they wished he wouldn't get into certain things that did cause trouble for himself or the *posada*. The Reyes children were taught English and Spanish from their father's collection of books. Reading, writing, business math, and the Christian faith were all topics covered by their father. Church was on Sundays too. Learning the arts, like crafts, folk dancing, time management, home care, gardening, and similar education from their mother and grandmother was also a part of their curriculum.

Rene eventually learned Italian after spending enough time with Ana's family. Ana's Italian father, Gilberto Lombardi, was fluent since that was his home "kingdom." Because of Rene's accelerated learning, she picked up the language quickly. The family was surprised at her gift of intelligence but didn't think too much about it since Ana mentioned Rene was always learning at home. Dr. Rameriz worked a lot at the clinic, helping anyone who came in needing medical care, regardless of his or her economic status or ability to pay. Gilberto was a laborer wherever he could find work. He was a fair skinned, blue-green eyed, and sandy-blond haired Italian man from the northern region. He had been a real estate developer and businessman in New York and had been well educated by his own father, a professor in Italy. He did not fit in with the common dark-haired, tanned-skinned men in Mexico, and he felt it among his co-workers. He was often excluded from gatherings after work by the men. Ana had shared about the outcast feelings towards her family from the locals the first day she met Rene, and her father was not exempt. He didn't speak Spanish. However, Dr. Rameriz went by her maiden name in Mexico to assimilate easier with the demographic.

Many times *Signore* Lombardi would come home feeling downtrodden and exhausted. He would find comfort in a bottle, like Uncle Tomás, but for different reasons. He wanted to still his ever thinking mind, being so under utilized in his current profession, and alcohol did that for him. He knew deep down that it was only a temporary solution for his problem. He did find that he did get more time at home with his daughters, and that was a positive for the family with the Doctor always at work. He was a silly drunk, so the family was never too hard on him for his habit. Once he threw a piece of pizza dough at Lidi while she was reading, as he drunkenly made one for his family at the outdoor pizza oven he fashioned in their yard. Making pizza seemed to relax him sometimes, and that was a skill his mother taught him, as she was a baker back home. Sometimes just getting into chopping ingredients helped him forget the troubles around him. One evening, he tossed a pizza into the oven so quickly, a coal had jumped out into a pile of leaves. Rene quickly went over to stomp out the fire with her feet, since he was unaware of what had happened. Ana had noticed what Rene did but quickly was distracted by her dogs barking into the bushes nearby to remember to ask any questions.

Learning about pizza was fun for Rene, since she'd never had it before meeting the Rameriz-Lombardi family. It quickly became her favorite food too. Collectively they called it the "*Amici* Pizza," because it was their meal among friends. Not to mention, the ingredients weren't expensive, and it was easy to make in a pinch. They would eat outdoors since there was more room for them to gather when guests came over. Ana would try not to be ashamed of her small rundown house that was far from the luxuries of her New York home. She would sometimes reminisce and tell Rene about the days where she didn't have to get Lidi's hand-me-downs and going to school on the Omni bus or horse drawn railway cars. There was even a cable powered railway on the Brooklyn Bridge running not long before the family came to Mexico. Ana also shared that it was for "family reasons" they came to Mexico. Rene didn't press her for answers, but she just figured she had secrets of her own just like herself. They both did their best to not give away those secrets just yet.

Now the girls were approaching womanhood by traditional standards, their 15th birthdays were coming up, and they too were changing. With Rene continuing a normal growth rate and only being a few inches taller than Ana when they met, the family went along with her being the same age as her friend. Naturally, Ana and Rene experienced hormonal changes, and their figures matured as well. Rene was a brawny looking teen and had muscle tone that no one seemed to know where it came from. Sure she was active and athletic outdoors, climbing trees, swimming, playing kickball and hiking with her parents, but that didn't seem to be all she did everyday. She ate a lot! It was as if she ran a marathon daily for her body to crave so many calories. It wasn't just in this reality that Rene seemed to live in, but another as well and these two worlds were coming to a head. This was more apparent with the violent outburst from this latest dream.

"Have you seen me move around before in my sleep?" Rene finally asked after a few moments passed as she recalled her dream.

"Eh, not really. Or not like THAT before anyway." Ana replied as she continued swimming around Rene, who was still stuck in her tracks in the river. Ana had gotten better about swimming in deeper water over the years and having a braver friend to encourage, even distract her from her fears, also helped.

"Well, you're the only one who ever sleeps with me, so there's no one else that would know," Rene muttered back with her mouth just above the water. Cristiano slept in their parent's room behind a room divider in his own little bed their father made him. Nana loved the privacy of her own room after a whole day spent with people in the *posada*. Some nights, she would start off laying with Rene talking about the day, saying their bedtime prayer, and eventually she would sneak off to her room when Rene fell asleep.

"Maybe I forgot to pray before bed last night," Rene told Ana with a phony smile to hopefully get her friend's mind off the incident. She then dove underwater to try to grab Ana's foot. Ana saw her coming and swam away, laughing and screaming. When Rene came up for air, Lidi and T.T. were there. Lidi had been watching Cristiana at home while Rene and Ana went off to the river.

"Hey, we gotta go to the clinic now Ana. T.T. says she's sick, and she keeps fake coughing! Let's go!" Lidi called out to Ana from the river's shore.

"Ugh. Okay!" Ana replied with a huff. "Are you coming, Ren?" Ana asked looking back at Rene, who was still swimming around but listening to the conversation.

"Oh, no. I gotta go home, my mama said she needs my help there today." Rene quickly replied. She had almost forgotten about her duties at home since her dream now occupied her thoughts. Ana nodded and sloshed her way out of the water toward her sandals. As the three sisters headed off towards the plaza, with a whine, Rene could hear Ana and Lidi arguing while each big sister held Cristiana's hands. Cristiana mentioned her ears were also hurting now. She didn't mean to eavesdrop, but sharp hearing was one of Rene's gifts.

As Rene began moving towards the river side to go home, a little lizard swimming nearby caught her eye.

What was that thing? I've never seen something like that swimming here before. Rene thought.

The little lizard then popped its head out of the water, and Rene saw part of its head was disfigured. Then some gills poked out of the sides of its head resembling a drawing in Mama Happy's "Book of Secrets" Nana carried with her.

An axolotl! How cute! How rare! Rene exclaimed in her head, as a surprised look took over her face. *Yuck, I'm not eating that thing, even if Mama Happy had a great recipe for it!* she also admitted to herself.

When it turned to face Rene, she noticed some prominent blue spots on its head in contrast to its pale body, but also that it had a missing eye.

Cristiano would love you too. But as a pet, not to eat. Rene chuckled as her internal dialog continued.

As the axolotl turned away and began to swim downstream slowly, Rene decided to follow it. Grabbing a floating log nearby helped her to glide along with the axolotl so she wouldn't be splashing too much. The little guy didn't seem afraid of her, which surprised Rene, because most of the time, it seemed as though any creatures in her vicinity would quickly vacate, feeling her strong presence, especially snakes. Ana always appreciated that but was never sure why it happened, as usual.

Following the axolotl, she approached an area of the river she and Ana had never ventured to before. The critter came to a stop along some rocks, at the shoreline still partially underwater. Rene studied it as she floated nearby. She traced his outlines with her finger in the air between them, committing his image to memory. The creature looked back at Rene as if he were just as curious about her, until a nearby hanging branch of leaves was caught by the wind and startled him away. Looking towards the branch, slightly cursing its existence; something else quickly caught Rene's eye. Something black, shining like glass amongst the river rocks underwater. Her eyes focused like a magnifying glass as she approached the area. As she felt around with her foot underwater, she felt the sharp edges of the rock.

Obsidian. Like from a volcano. Maybe Popo. Rene confirmed her thought of that shiny black rock to herself.

Popo was the nickname of the volcano not far away. Her father would point out different rocks, plants, and other such things when they would take their hikes. Cristiano was often strapped on his back when he was a baby and came along too. Besides the fact that they also had miners in the family, they loved rocks, and Rene loved learning about earth sciences since she loved the outdoors. Nana Maria's father and brothers were miners, and Rene's twin uncles she called "Nino and Nano" now managed that old mine in the next state over. Just then, another gust of wind again hit the branches that startled her axolotl friend moments ago. This time Rene noticed something else behind the branches in the hillside.

More obsidian? Rene questioned as she moved the branches out of the way to get a better look.

"A CAVE!" Rene gasped.

Her eyes went bright green, as curiosity and excitement filled her mind. She carefully parted the branches and went inside. She ran her hand over the side of the cave wall, and a chunk of obsidian broke off into it.

Opps! Rene thought but quickly added, *Maybe I better hold onto this just in case.*

Further into the cave, she discovered that it was actually a tunnel. Forgetting all about getting back to the *posada*, Rene threw caution to the wind and followed the tunnel further into the hillside, rock in hand. Rene bounced along on the rocks underwater below, nicking her waterlogged, wrinkly feet here and there on other fallen pieces of obsidian. She was just tall enough to keep her head out of water as she bounced along and paddled with her one free hand. As the light from outside began to fade, she grew slightly worried but still focused on learning where this led. Rene continued on feeling drawn to something there as she went deeper into the tunnel.

Ana wouldn't ever appreciate this dark water, Rene thought, laughing nervously.

Suddenly torches embedded into the walls lit with a **POOF!** It was much like what the candles at home did when she was little and woke up emotional. The tunnel was now lit ahead of her, and the ceiling of the cave grew higher the further she went in, and the water slowly became shallower. A ledge along the wall also formed as she continued on. It appeared to have been carved out by someone long ago since the obsidian was not present here.

I wonder if this was here since the war like the other tunnels the soldiers used here in Puebla? Rene asked herself.

After what felt like an eternity following the narrow tunnel, the ledge finally opened up wide enough for her to climb out of the water. Hauling herself onto the ledge, she noticed a small, metal barred door at the base of the wall she faced.

Now where does this go!? Rene anxiously inquired, her mind filled with many questions now.

She crawled up to the door and sat on her knees. She set her rock down and grabbed the bars to give the door a shake to hopefully open it. **CLANG**! The door broke off the hinges, which seemed to be no match for Rene's current strength.

Ana's lucky I didn't break her ribs when I punched her last night! Rene thought in fear for her friend looking down at the little door in her hands.

She gently placed the grate on the floor, wondering if anyone could have heard what she had done. Picking her rock back up, she poked her head into the small doorway as more sconces lit up the new room. After a quick scan of the area, Rene proceeded to crawl into the room. A small, wooden desk sat in the corner with a single chair, and across the room was a staircase that led to a large wooden door with metal details and a handle. As Rene walked around the room, she felt curious dips and gaps in the floor below her bare feet that were now quickly going back to normal. She hustled to the stairs to get a look at the room as a whole and saw that there were carvings and possible designs she was unfamiliar with throughout the stone floor and some of the walls. Overwhelmed with the new discoveries and being unable to contain the questions filling her mind, Rene quickly turned around to try the door handle.

I need to get out of this dungeon. Mama is going to be mad! She told herself as anxiety now built up inside her. She rattled the lever. LOCKED.

"Shoot! I don't want to go back around!" Rene whined out loud, deciding to give the door another try. As she reached for the handle, the lock suddenly came undone, and the handle began to creak. She gathered that the handle was being controlled by someone on the other side, as she heard heavy breathing and shoes shuffling along the floor.

Alerted, Rene got into her fighting stance, holding her rock up ready to strike as the door slowly began to open. Her heart was pounding, and her eyes lit to their brightest green yet.

CHAPTER 6
Quinceañera

"Aye, *Mija*, you scared me!" The small nun in robes yelped, clutching a rosary in her hand. She let go of the door and let out a large sigh, as she looked down and mumbled something as she raised the cross around her neck to kiss it.

"I'm sorry, Sister." Rene quickly replied, touching the nun's arm gently. "I followed the river underground to get here." She quickly went on to explain.

The nun looked at Rene's hand on her arm and stopped breathing for a moment. She felt like she nearly had a heart attack seeing Rene at the door with her bright green eyes looking back at her. But as Rene's hand touched her arm on top of her robes, she immediately felt heat flow through her body, and her heart regulated back to normal from the pounding fear. Rene then relaxed too, and her eyes went back to the natural earth toned hazel color.

"Who are you?" The woman slowly asked Rene, looking at her in the eyes as the colors changed.

Ana had never noticed Rene's drastic eye color change over the years. She seemed to have a problem keeping focused on things which limited her eye contact with Rene or was always distracted with something else immediately. She was just about as busy body and mind as Rene, but the nun here before her noticed it right away.

"I'm Rene Reyes," Rene responded with her own hint of curiosity. "Javier and Julia's daughter. We have the *posada* outside of town, and the Tesoros shop in the plaza—" Rene shared before the woman interjected.

"I have no record of a daughter for Reyes, only a son." The nun quickly noted from memory. Rene remained quiet for a moment, unsure what to say next. "I keep the records of the births and deaths here in the city. Your family are patrons here, *Mija*. I know," she continued.

Rene cut in finally and said, "I'm not um..."

"...of this world?" the nun finished the sentence for Rene.

Rene's eyes widened and began to light up again. *How could she know? We didn't tell anyone!* she thought to herself.

"It's okay. Your secret's safe with me," the nun whispered as she placed her hand on Rene's shoulder to ease her growing anxiety. Rene's eyes relaxed, and she let out a sigh of relief.

"But how did you know?" Rene questioned, still in shock.

"Your eyes told me. There was something exceptional about how they changed so quickly from colors of the earth to the brighter green. When you touched my arm, my fear fled from me, and my heart stopped pounding. That's a strong gift, *Mija*." The woman shared with a smile.

"We don't talk about it outside the family, *Señora*. Privacy is important to us. I know I'm different, but I don't want to be treated that way," Rene added with a sense of fear.

"You have nothing to fear here. I sense great power in you, and I'm sure whoever sent you here will guard this secret carefully," the woman assured Rene, as she motioned the sign of the cross across her head, shoulders, and heart.

"Thank you, *Señora*. That is good to hear," Rene said graciously, bowing her head at the woman.

"I'm Sister Esther Maria, *Niña*. Rene was your name again?" Esther inquired.

"*Sí*. Rene, *Señora*, or Ren for short," Rene replied with a small smile.

"Please, call me Esther, *Amada*," Esther quickly corrected Rene, smiling back.

The two spoke a while there inside what turned out to be the *Catedral de Puebla*. Esther gave Rene a quick tour and history of the church and grounds. She also let Rene know that she could and should come see her anytime she wanted. Esther let Rene know that it would be her honor to assist her and serve her in any way she could. Rene was most grateful for this news. Her parents were very busy and had traveled much for Cristiano's doctor visits in the past four years. She would appreciate a knowledgeable woman such as Esther to be another guidance figure in her life.

Rene also let Esther know that she had grown a little distant from her mother too ever since her little brother had come. She revealed how she knew beforehand that one of his eyes would be different and had some regret about sharing that. Though Julia was a woman of God and had faith, she had not always been brought up in the environment where the strength and power of Jesus was with them whenever it was called upon. In short, Rene's mother was a worrier and her father was her go to for all her questions and shared her issues or concerns with. She felt like her mother could not handle those burdens without panic setting in. Rene just stopped sharing with her mother emotionally, and that weighed heavy on Rene's heart knowing she and her mother could not have that kind of intimate relationship. It was troubling for her. Esther let Rene know that she would be praying for her mother and that this rift would heal soon. The two kissed each other reverently on each side of their faces like family and said goodbye.

Rene then bolted home as fast as she could, concerned that she had gotten sidetracked with the findings of the cave, tour, and other things with Esther. She ran up to the front door of the *posada*, quickly composed herself, and let herself in the door. *Just be cool Rene, time to get to work.* she told herself as she marched in the house ready to serve the incoming guests. "Rene! *Aye*, there you are," Julia said with a sigh of relief, as she came around the corner holding little Christiano's hand. "Did you have fun with your friend?"

"Yes, Mama. Mr. Lombarbi made pizza again. I love pizza!" Rene replied with a smile, relieved her mother wasn't in complete panic.

"Oh good, *Niña*. I'm glad you're home. Here, can you take Christiano for me really quick; he's getting into things while we're in the kitchen. We have flour all over the floor," Julia asked anxiously, placing Christiano's hand in Rene's. Rene noticed flour on her little brother's hands now.

"Okay, Mama." Rene agreed with a chuckle as she began to dust off Cristiano's hand.

"*Aye*, Rene, we're very busy today. You know we are starting to plan for your quinceanera coming up. My family will be coming from the big city, and Ernestina has asked to come stay with your cousin Alana, too," Julia explained.

"Nina is coming?!" Rene interjected excitedly hearing her aunt would be coming to visit.

"Yes. She wants to get away for a while and I don't blame her," Julia finished with a hint of stress, disguised behind a laugh as she rushed off.

"Well, we haven't seen them in a while." Rene said looking down at Cristiano who had been staring out at the patio watching some birds coming and going. One bird caught Rene's eye, reminding her of Reina, making her heart flutter and remember their happy days together in Córdoba.

"Can we go outside?" Cristiano mumbled to his sister. She snapped out of her childhood memories of her and her little bird friend, nodded, and let Cris lead the way outdoors.

    Before they knew it, November 1st was here, and the excitement in the house was at its highest. It was *Dia de los Muertos* and the day of Rene's *quinceañera*. Julia's family arrived at the *posada* a few days before, and though there always seemed to be some sort of tension in the family, they did come together to help each other out, especially Ernestina. She was

Julia's only sister, and she was 15 years younger. She had come to stay at the *posada* a couple years ago and was very helpful when Julia had gone away for Cristiano's doctor appointments and glass eye fittings. Rene considered her as more of an older sister than an aunt too. Though Rene had not yet been baptized at the church, she called her Nina because she would be her godmother one day.

Rene's baptism took place shortly after Ernestina's arrival at the *Catedral*. Uncle Arsenio would be her godfather since Rene had started calling him Nino, of course. He was Javier's oldest of his younger brothers. Even though he was a twin, he came out first. Rene had a hard time saying Arsenio so "Nino" became his nickname anyway. His twin, Adriano got a nickname too; "Nano." They all very much loved their nicknames from Rene, except Tomás. She called him "Toe," but as soon as Rene was able, he begged her to just call him by his whole name because he thought feet were gross.

Sister Esther, of course assisted the deacon and priest at the small baptism held a few days before the party. Since Rene wasn't baptized as an infant, they had brought in a horse's trough for Rene to get into at the altar. There, in her brown robe as she kneeled down in the steel trough, the deacon poured water over her head to complete the sacrament with her family surrounding her. Because of Cristiano's eye condition, Javier and Julia had him baptized after Dr. Rameriz noticed an issue. Besides, the Reyes' had gone off to Córdoba in a hurry to raise Rene. Who had time for a baptism at that time?

Today was a big day being both *Dia de los Muertos* and Rene's *quinceañera*. It was the talk of the village. Her mother and father invited everyone they knew, even some they didn't know as well.

The Reyes' also hired the *Figueroa Cocineras* to help with the cooking, since well over 150 people agreed to come to the celebration. Nana Maria was also thankful for the help. Cooking for an army sized guestlist was not something Maria was looking forward to that day, since Maria's older brother and sister came into town with their families from Sonora. Maria still called it Sonora opposed to Alta California- even though the territory had been lost to the United States years ago. She was happy to have time to visit with her own siblings she didn't see that often.

Hiring the *Cocineras* also freed up the Reyes for the decorating, which they all always enjoyed. Javier and his brothers had spent the last two weeks repainting the arches, trim, and walls facing the courtyard a fresh tan and white. Extra wooden tables and chairs were placed in the main courtyard outside the patio. Fresh, white tablecloths and arrangements of red flowers and roses and dozens of golden painted candles decorated the table tops. Young jacaranda trees were also placed around the courtyard, giving an extra splash of color to the ambiance. The best glasses were brought out for the guests, along with plates and utensils that were left in the home from the royal family that lived there long before. Ana even spent time with Julia painting some new plates for the head table prior to the event. With Rene's encouragement, Ana even painted the wall of the staircase landing a colorful floral design to be a sort of backdrop behind Rene as she would make her entrance to the party and greet her guests. Rene had found every opportunity for her friend to use her creative and artistic talents, which Ana appreciated.

    Rene would be dressed in a red gown they had custom-made under the direction of Julia. The sleeves were a sheer lace fabric with floral designs; the bodice and skirt were made of layers of silk-like fabric. A full petticoat gave the dress a lofty look, while a white and gold sash made from her baby blanket from her arrival was put around her waist. Julia also managed to find some fancy boots for Rene, with a conservative heel and pointed toe in a similar red color as her dress. Boots seemed to be the only kind of shoes Rene agreed to wear over the past couple years. She'd come home with a few scars on her feet from playing kickball, so Julia insisted she'd wear shoes a little more often. Rene was not excited to be getting dressed up today. She was very tomboy-like, not only because Javier raised her like he and his brothers were raised, but also because she just preferred the comfort of loose clothes since she was so active and muscular.

Ana, on the other hand, appreciated the pampering and elegant dress she would get to wear alongside Rene for the event. The Reyes family had custom dresses made for all the girls that were to be a part of the ceremony, all of which were Rene's cousins and distant cousins, aside from Ana. Some she didn't know all that well, but Rene had heard about them living up there in the New Mexico territory.

"I can't wait to get married one day," Ana shared ardently as she unbraided her hair next to Rene before the party officially began. Rene just smiled back at Ana with a quiet chuckle.

"I'm not getting married though. But yeah, I guess it's not so bad getting dressed up sometimes," Rene replied as she unbraided her own hair.

"Oh my God! I look like a Lion!" Ana announced with dread. She quickly turned away from the mirror to look at Rene, put her hands up, and added a "ROAR!" Rene swung back off the bench seat she sat on and fell back into the wood floor laughing hysterically. Ana also joined in laughing, as tears set in from laughing so hard at herself.

"Maybe your hair was curly enough before the braids," Rene confessed as she sat up and clutched her chest to catch her breath. Ana was gripping at her hair trying to pull it straight, nervously laughing. Rene stood and made her way over to Ana to help her friend's hair fiasco. "Let's just tie it back," Rene suggested, pulling the ribbon from her final braid to tie back Ana's mane. In the mirror, Ana watched Rene work her magic as she styled her hair and molded some curls in order around her face. Ana smiled in approval but quickly looked down to her hands in her lap.

"My mom never has time to help with my hair, being a doctor and all. She works so much," Ana confessed as her eyes began to water.

"I know, Ana. Thank God for friends to help out though, right?" Rene whispered as she rested her hand on her friend's shoulder to calm her.

"Yes. I'm grateful for friends," Ana replied, looking up with watery eyes into the mirror at Rene's reflection with a smile.

Just then, Rene's bedroom door opened abruptly as Christiano and Alana ran in ahead of Aunt Ernestina, who was carrying Rene's gown. She was followed by Julia and Nana Maria, who were holding up a gown for Ana. Rene's gown and sash fit her beautifully, and she did her best to appreciate it in front of her mother, who was clearly more excited about it than she was.

"I feel like I'm wearing an umbrella, Mama," Rene joked. "I look like a cake!"

"You're fine, *Mija*," Julia quickly added. "No, you look beautiful."

"You look like a pretty cupcake, Rene!" Ana added with a smile, as Ernestina helped lace up Ana's dress. "Those were my favorite in New York."

As the girls were finally dressed, Javier entered the room with a small treasure box in his hands.

"We've been waiting a long time to give you this, *Amor*." Javier announced with a smile, as he approached his daughter.

Rene slowly opened the latch of the box, and the lid of the box cracked open. Rene's eyes lit up in awe. The light in her bedroom shone upon a beautiful, petite, crown with red dazzling rubies and brilliant diamonds. Beside it was another small wooden box, beautifully carved with leaf details.

"Your Uncles Adriano and Arsenio had this put together for you. They are sorry they couldn't be here tonight for the party. The mine had a cave in, and they are making sure everyone gets out safely," Javier shared, as Rene's eyes slowly relaxed, blinking as she studied the crown.

"Wow, *Papi*. It's beautiful," she said humbly. "But what is this?" She quickly asked as she pointed at the little box. Julia, who was standing nearby, picked up the box and began to open it.

"This is from your father and I, Rene," Julia shared with a smile.

As the lid was removed from the box, Rene saw a shiny, golden-winged charm. Between the wings, it was adorned with a single fiery-colored opal stone. The top and base of the opal was encrusted with tiny, black obsidian stones. The crown of the charm was adorned with three bright green gems. As Julia lifted the charm, Rene saw a gold chain follow behind it. Her eyes locked on the precious gift from her parents.

"It's to honor Reina. We thought it shined just like her," Julia shared as she motioned for Rene to turn so she could put the necklace on her daughter's neck. "Every stone here has a power behind it they say, but it is only the wearer that gives it any energy. You know this."

Rene nodded as she traced the wings and stones with her finger against her collarbone as her mother latched the necklace's clasp. Once the necklace was secure, Rene walked over to the mirror to look at its reflection as she sat back down on the bench.

"It's the best part of this outfit. Thank you. I love it," Rene said as she smiled with gratitude.

"But tonight you ARE Reina, *Mija*," Javier added, as he placed the crown of jewels on her head as Nina helped position her wavy hair around the crown.

"Now remember to sit up straight with your shoulders back, Rene. Stand proud with this crown on your head, even when you're not wearing it," Javier instructed, as he looked at his daughter's reflection with pride.

The celebration at the *posada* was the event of the decade. Everything went as planned. Even Ana's minor slip on the staircase for the grand entrance was expected, but all eyes were thankfully on Rene.

As Rene moved about the party thanking her family for attending she stayed as poised as possible, hauling around her dress. She reminded herself that many family members had faced greater troubles in their travels to be there than she had wearing that dress. Some members she hadn't seen in a while since they lived far away, and as her parents traveled often in recent years, they hadn't been invited to visit. Still, with Rene's powerful memory, she was able to remember everyone of course. If not, she'd overheard their names before arriving at their tables with her acute hearing abilities.

As she quickly turned from one table to the next greeting people, she sensed someone coming towards her quickly. Her body temperature on her arms and neck quickly rose, alerting her.

"Whoah!" Rene yelped as a young man carrying a tray of plates nearly crashed into her. She reached out to grab the tray, stopping it from spilling on her and the server. Her eyes quickly flashed green but faded once the situation was corrected.

"I'm sorry, Rene!" The boy quickly apologized. "I guess I was rushing around so quickly I didn't check where it was going. Forgive me," he finished.

"I'm okay. Everything is fine," Rene said with a smile and a gentle bow towards the boy so as to not make eye contact. Sensing a familiar strain in her eyes, she knew her eyes had changed colors and excused herself from the party as gracefully as possible, just in case.

  Later that evening, as Rene and Ana sat at the head table for dessert, Ana brought up the "almost" accident. "So. Carlos almost ruined your night! Yikes," she recalled with terror, straightening out Rene's gown next to her as they sat.

"Who did what?" Rene quickly questioned Ana looking confused.

"Carlos. The young *cameriere* who almost crashed into you out there? Earlier? I thought this dress was finished!" Ana chatted on, continuing to adjust Rene's dress.

"Oh, that's his name? How do you know? Why do you know everyone?" Rene laughed as she swatted Ana's hands away, stopping Ana from moving her dress around anymore.
"My mom is the doctor… recall? I see everyone come in and see their names when I'm there with the paperwork?" Ana added. "I think he's kinda cute. No serious health issues, just seems sad a lot."

Ana laughed nervously but went on to nudge Rene, who'd spotted Carlos off in the distance. He was a young man, no more than a few years older than the girls. He had brown, wavy hair, and was slightly taller than Rene. He was carrying a tray of desserts, serving the guests towards the back of the courtyard.

"Great. Are you gonna marry him?" Rene taunted back with a laugh, nudging Ana back. Ana always seemed to have a new love interest these days, it seemed.

"Nah. I like the *chiaro* type. Sooo… maybe you will!" Ana replied with a chuckle, as she went back to eating her cake.

Rene just rolled her eyes and went back to eating her cake as well. Not putting any weight into Ana's crazy thought, she dusted some crumbs off her sash and wondered for a moment about her own past. She had sometimes wondered more about that than her future.

CHAPTER 7
Uninvited

November 1, 1898 10:45pm

"I don't know why I let you drag me out for another party tonight. I had enough already at the *posada* didn't you?" Rene gently complained towards Ana as they headed home from the plaza.

"It's *Dia de los Muertos*! It's fun to party. Don't act like an old lady or I'll call you Lidi!" Ana laughed. "I wasn't going to dance with any of your cousins so… the plaza is where we needed to go. We always go!" Ana retorted, her happiness then seemed to fade as she looked back at Rene.

"I know but, my feet were dying wearing those shoes mama had me wear, and with that 100 pound dress... I mean good thing I put these boots on, but ugh," Rene whined back. She had changed into another less formal dress her mother had put aside for special occasions. Julia took advantage of any occasion to dress her daughter up since she usually insisted on dressing like she borrowed her father's clothes on a regular basis.

"I just want to forget about Finn and find someone new," Ana added, sounding even more grief stricken now.

"Ugh. Finn. He was no good, Ana. I felt it when we all hung out that first day," Rene recalled as the memory flashed through her mind, reaffirming her judgment.

"You don't like anyone, Rene. Well, boys I mean," Ana complained back.

"They're not a priority for me. That's all. I'm happy just having you and some of the others to hang out with. Boys? Romance? Bleh. Maybe when I'm done with my studies," Rene stated with confidence.

The air suddenly grew thick and colder on the walk home. Ana shivered suddenly and began to cry, bringing her hands to her face.

"Oh don't cry, you'll ruin your gloves and your face paint!" Rene warned, as she grabbed Ana's shoulders and tried to console her friend.

Rene patted her friends back and tried offering her some kind words and wisdom as they walked back to the *posada*. As they approached the cemetery along the way, something suddenly triggered Rene's protective instincts.

Rene's eyes flashed green, and suddenly, a shadowy figure flew right at her and Ana. Rene acted quickly and pushed Ana away, causing her to fall back and land on her behind in confusion near the border of the cemetery.

    The world around Rene seemed to dissipate, as she and the demon spirit engaged in what seemed like another realm. It was a woman-like creature floating above the ground, almost legless. It blurred where the bottom of her legs and feet would've been. Her hair was wild, uneven and uncared for, and her teeth were jagged and yellowed. She was lean but muscular in stature and had large hands with long, claw-like nails. Her clothes were just as hacked looking as her hair, and behind her back were large black wings. A tiny skull hung from her waist.

Rene noted all these details in her mind just as a ball of fire formed in one of the demon's hands. With an evil cackle, the woman threw the flame at Rene, but with her gift of speed and anticipation, Rene evaded the fire ball's path with a sideways tumble and caught it with her bare hand, absorbing the flames. Suddenly, a memory of this creature flashed through her mind, distracting her thoughts from the redness pulsing in her hand now.

I've seen you in a dream! Rene exclaimed to herself. *How are you here?*

The two proceeded to fight each other savagely. They moved with such speed and intensity in their quarrel that a cloud of dust formed around them. It was the flying dust from the fight catching in the dense cold air that made Rene think she was in another realm. However it wasn't the case. The atmosphere was actually impairing Ana from seeing much of what was going on. She tried to call out to Rene but was never answered by her friend. Ana cowered in fear as she tried hiding by a pillar bordering the cemetery. She anxiously waited for the fight to end and the dust to settle.

The enemies fought tirelessly on that dark barren road to the *posada*. Though Rene's various gifts assisted her in battle, this was her first quarrel in this reality. Only in her dreams had she ever fought anyone, and there she wasn't wearing a party dress. There she would be in a native garb with a full feathered headdress, shield, and staff to help her fight, but not here.

She scrambled as swiftly as one possibly could in her gown and boots. Rene quickly scanned the grounds and found a large jagged stone. She finally caught a break after dodging the spirit's oncoming attack and gave the woman a blunt kick to the head with the heel of her boot, causing her to fall to the ground. She ran up a crooked tree and kicked off its trunk, launching her into the air, where Ana finally caught a glimpse of Rene. It had seemed like forever not knowing what was going on behind the dust cloud. She saw Rene's arm was cocked back with the stone in hand winding up for her final blow to defeat the creature. Ana screamed as she hid behind her hands reactively. On the inside, she was amazed and filled with awe as to why her friend seemed to have the fighting capacity of a trained ninja she'd read about in a book once. Rene came down with her stone weapon, as if she were a pile driving something into the ground, breaking the clay-laden path they were previously walking along. Ana felt the ground rumble as a pained scream escaped the dust cloud and silenced in the air.

The air quickly cleared as Rene held the position with her hand on the ground bent down on one knee as the shadow woman faded away beneath her. Rene whispered something at the ground where she knelt and shook her head, snapping out of the trance she had been in. The stone was lodged down into the clay path now where the demon once laid. Ana quickly jumped up and ran for her friend, who seemed half confused about what just happened. Ana clutched Rene's arm, lifting her hand from the ground.

"Ren! What was that?" Ana questioned with a shaky voice as she held onto her friend. Rene's eyes faded back to their peaceful color state as she took a deep breath and looked over at her friend.

"I have a family secret too, Ana. Can I tell you back at home?" Rene quickly replied as calmly as possible. She stood up and dusted herself off quickly and examined her hand that had caught the ball of fire moments ago. It was red but didn't hurt much.

"I never thought I'd say this but- let's run!" Ana added anxiously. As Rene nodded back, the two turned and bolted for Rene's house up the street.

When the two approached the house door they further composed themselves before entering, looking over each other to make sure nothing was out of the ordinary. Rene immediately caught her breath, as Ana still heaved on. She had seemed to have trouble breathing.

"It's asthma... Ma said... Hang on," Ana breathed, as she cupped her mouth with her hands and took in deep gulps of air.

"Ok, just tell my father we danced a lot," Rene said as she shook her injured hand at her side. It felt like it had gone to sleep, and sparks coursed through her hand. She opened and closed her hand, and the redness faded a little more as Ana finally controlled her breath enough to enter the house.

As the girls entered the front door, Javier looked up with tired eyes from his book lowering his glasses. He was sitting in a big chair in the *posada* lobby waiting for the girls to return home. Rene smiled and smoothly hid her hand behind her back as she approached her father, Ana followed her lead.

"Hi, *Papi*." Rene greeted her father quickly, giving him a kiss on the cheek.

"*Señor* Reyes," Ana chimed in kindly as she nodded her head in a bow. "Thanks for having me over again. I do love your house," Ana added, half suspiciously. Javier nodded back in acknowledgement.

"We're happy to have you again, Ana," he replied with a tired smile, half hidden by his mustache as he stood from his chair, closing the book he had been reading. "Glad you girls are home on time. Thank you," he said with a tired, cracking voice.

As the girls slowly turned to continue down the hall, Rene shyly waved on Ana to go to her room ahead of her. Rene had noticed a concerned look on her father's face, and she knew she would have to clear that up. Also trying to avoid the conversation, Rene went over to give her father another peck on the cheek goodnight when Javier suddenly leaned to the side to look at Rene's hidden hands.

"What happened here?" Javier gently questioned.

"Can I tell you tomorrow, *Papi*?" Rene quickly answered as she watched Ana disappear. Javier sighed heavily and thought for a moment before answering.

"Yes, *Mija*. As long as you're ok," he finally replied as he stood from his chair.

"Yes. I'm okay," Rene added quickly but honestly, and Javier nodded in approval. Rene smiled and went ahead with kissing his cheek goodnight.

Ana laid on Rene's bed with her eyes wide open, staring up at the ceiling when she finally motioned with her hands at the sides of her head, quickly whipping them outward adding an explosion noise. ***BOOM!***

"My mind exploded, Ren. *Che figo*! Your family secret is way better than mine," she added with a hint of shame.

"No one has the exact same family stories, Ana. I'm sure yours is alright too," Rene interjected, lying next to Ana also staring at the ceiling.

"No, it's not. It's nothing like yours," Ana quickly replied, covering her face with her hands rolling onto her side away from Rene.

"You can tell me if you want, Ana. I'm your friend no matter what," Rene assured her friend as she sat up to look at her, placing her hand on Ana's arm. Ana took her hands off her face as she still faced toward the bedroom wall, grabbing the blankets, and pulling them up to her chin with both hands slowly. Rene grew concerned.

"What happened? Tell me please?" Rene questioned kindly, wondering what could have happened to her dear, funny friend.

"My uncles touched me," Ana finally muttered with a shaky voice, "that's why we left New York." Tears welled up in the corner of her eye, pooling up by her small nose as she lay facing the wall.

Rene stayed quiet as her mind raced hoping Ana would go on. What did she mean by "touched"?

"I didn't know what was wrong until my ma told me at her office one day," Ana continued on, sniffling as the tears began to roll off her face down onto her pillow. "They said they were playing Doctor, like my ma. But mama never touched me down there, and I asked her why not, because her brothers did. To me and Lidi." Ana cried softly and sniffed loudly as she brought the blankets up to wipe her tears. Rene sat there in confusion and fear for her friend, unsure what to do, but kept listening.

"My mom said only grown up ladies who are going to have babies get checked down there, not little girls. One of my uncles has a mental problem, so my parents felt bad and didn't want anything to happen to him. Like being sent away somewhere to an institution or worse. So we just left as soon as my parents settled everything and came to Mexico," Ana blubbered as slowly as she could to hopefully make some sense to her friend.

Ana went on to say how she blamed herself for ever saying anything to make her family leave New York, for making her mother fight with her family and her own husband. Also, how Lidi still never wants to speak of it and buries the secret deep down and covers her body a lot with clothes. Her mom was sad to leave her family and her younger brothers she helped raise since her parents died in Puerto Rico. Gilberto insisted they leave to protect the girls and hopefully find a less demanding doctor position, but where they were sorely needed and hopefully more appreciated in a place like Mexico.

"I wish I could just forget it ever happened, Ren. I hate getting flashbacks and feeling hopeless. Not being able to talk about it with anyone doesn't help either," Ana finished.

"Yeah. I'd want to forget something like that too, Ana, but I'm glad you guys came here because that's been the best thing that happened to me. You're like a sister to me," Rene added with a smile as she continued to kneel at her friend's side.

Ana sat up and hugged Rene firmly as Rene awkwardly hugged her back. Rene wasn't much of the hugging type unless it came to hugging her Nana. She did her best to comfort her friend, especially now after hearing about the struggles she and her family had faced.

"We can try to pray about forgetting that memory, Ana. I'm sure God can help heal you," Rene added.

"Oh my God! Can you heal me?" Ana quickly pulled back and asked her friend with a serious tone, and her eyes widened as she smiled.

"Uh. Not that I know of. I just heal myself for now, but that just happens on its own," Rene laughed, looking at her hand she injured earlier now healed.

"*Mannaggia!*" Ana exclaimed disappointedly with a chuckle, snapping her fingers together.

"Sorry. I'll work on it though," Rene added with a smile.

How do I heal a mind? Rene asked herself after the two settled into bed to finally go to sleep. *I'll go ask Esther tomorrow.* She thought as she closed her eyes at last.

The next day, the girls enjoyed breakfast prepared by Nana Maria. Since it had been a late night and early morning rise to get to work that day, Rene thought they could ask for some coffee.

"Coffee, *Mija*? Well, I guess you're a woman now; here I'll get you some," Maria offered, getting up from the table to serve the girls. She added milk and sugar to their cups and brought them back to the table.

Rene grabbed her cup with both hands, again unbothered by the heat of the coffee, and took a big whiff and drank. "I'm gonna smell like *Papi* now," she laughed.

Ana carefully lifted her cup by the handle and took a slow sip. "I like the sugar part… what else is that I taste, Nana?" Ana asked.

"*Canela*, Ana," Maria answered with a wink. "That's the secret ingredient in this house. Mama Happy knows," she added with a smile as she sipped her coffee. Rene chuckled and shook her finger at Ana.

The girls finished their breakfast and coffee feeling more energized. They thanked Nana Maria and hurried off into town.

As they approached the plaza, Rene spotted Esther walking around the outside of the *Catedral*. She seemed to be pointing and taking mental notes looking at the surroundings.

Rene said goodbye to Ana and told her she'd see her later. Ana nodded and waved off her friend sprinting away.

"Sister Esther! Good morning!" Rene called out waving as Esther reached for the front door. Stopping in her tracks, Esther turned towards the voice, noticing the fiery red streaks in Rene's hair shining in the sunlight. Refocusing her gaze onto Rene's face she recognized her young *comadre*. The two greeted each other and entered the church. Sensing some anxiety in Rene, Esther cut to the chase for this early morning visit.

"*Hija*, is something troubling you?" Ester questioned looking Rene in the eyes.

"How did you know?" Rene quickly asked.

"Women's intuition, *Mija*," Esther answered with a smile as she patted the side of Rene's arm. "Even everyday people have helpful gifts from our Lord if they work on them," she added with a smile.

"*Sí, Señora.*" Rene smiled in agreement. "Well a couple of things. I need to learn how to heal a mind, and I also need to know about… spirits." Rene finished as she eagerly waited for an answer. She stared into Esther's eyes as if she were trying to read her mind to get the answer sooner.

"I see," Esther replied as the wheels in her mind turned as if an internal library in her were being accessed. Rene's father always told her about how the human mind, too, was like a large *catedral*, how many times people do not push their knowledge to fill but to only 10% of its potential. Esther was not one of these people. She was educated, even self-taught too.

"These are a couple things I've spent years studying about the human mind, here at the church and outside the church. There is no... one simple answer to give, I'm afraid. But I can help you learn as I did in time, okay?" Esther offered.

Doing her best not to become disappointed that there wasn't a quick fix for her best friend, she went on to ask again about the spirits. She told Esther how she encountered a spirit on her way home from the plaza last night and how it resembled a figure she had only fought in her mind or dreams before then.

When Rene recalled the fight with the spirit, Esther gasped and clutched the rosary hanging from her robes with one hand. She quickly whispered something under her breath and kissed the rosary and looked heavenward.

"Is that bad, Sister?" Rene asked concernedly as one of her eyebrows perplexed.

"No, Rene. We already know you're here on a mission from the Lord. You will face things we don't all have the honor to do in a way. Do you know what this spirit looked like?" Esther calmly asked.

Just then, footsteps came up behind Rene, and a familiar voice interjected. "Yes, I'd like to know what it looked like too, *Mija*."

Rene's hairs on her arm stood up and her eyes widened, as she slowly turned to see who it was.

CHAPTER 8
A History

Rene slowly turned to face the voice that came from behind her. It was her father, Javier. He had risen early that morning, as usual, and came to the church for confession and prayer as he sometimes did throughout the week.

"*Papi…*" Rene gasped.

"Good morning, *Hija*. Good morning, *Sorella*," Javier said with a suspicious smile at Rene, nodding reverently towards Esther. "It's a good morning for a confession it seems," he added, his eyes locked back on Rene.

"*Sí, Papi,*" Rene agreed, bowing her head at her father slowly. "*Comadre* Esther told me that I could visit anytime…" Rene tried to continue, but her father cut her off, raising his hand up to stop her.

"Rene, Esther is a wise woman and good counsel. I'm glad you've found refuge here," Javier interjected calmly.

She was relieved her father was not upset about her presence at the church with Esther. The three of them agreed to go to one of the office rooms in the church to listen to Rene's story of the spirit encounter she had with Ana last night. She explained that it had not been the first time she had encountered this woman, as she had dreamt of her a few months earlier when she slept over at Ana's. She told her *comadre* and father about punching her friend in the chest while she was asleep and not remembering the occurrence the next morning till Ana reminded her at the river. She then finally went into the fight to protect Ana last night with that same woman.

Rene explained that she had first felt an aggressive presence approaching her and Ana as they came near the cemetery on the walk home from the plaza. She was consoling her friend about a broken relationship when she sensed the energy and pushed her friend aside. She shared the figure was visible to only her because Ana could not see anyone else there she later admitted. Perhaps it was the cloud of dust that surrounded her and the evil spirit, but Ana thought Rene was fighting someone imaginary. Deep down, Rene felt that Ana was also afraid and may have kept her eyes closed as she hid behind a pillar by the cemetery. Rene recalled the event was like being in her dream, as if she were in a different dark realm altogether. The reality of the world around her and the cemetery had disappeared into mist. In her dreams, she would be dressed in a native garb with a feathered headdress of a bird, carrying a shield and staff. There, a rigid shell hung at her side that she applied her hand into to fight the spirit, but last night she had found a large stone to fight with in this reality as she flung around her dress.

She told her father and her *comadre* that the spirit had green eyes but glowed red. She appeared to be floating above the ground with no appearance of actual legs. The presence of dark wings on her back helped the spirit move swiftly, as Rene countered instinctively and found her opportunities to strike her or dodge her advances.

"I was lucky she didn't hit me, *Papi*. Once she threw a ball of fire at me, but I was able to catch and absorb the flames. She didn't like that," Rene explained.

"*La Lechuza,*" Esther gasped, signing the cross across herself again.

"The owl witch, *Sí*," Javier agreed.

"Don't tell Mama," Rene quickly added, looking at her father with concern. Javier looked back at Rene waiting for an explanation, his eyebrow perplexed.

"She worries, *Papi*. I can't do that to her," Rene pleaded looking down at her hands in her lap.

"What will happen when she sees you with marks or bruises on you, Rene?" Javier questioned.

"She hasn't noticed them so far. She's had enough troubles with Cristiano. You have too. But you seem to keep it together more. Mama is a different story," Rene argued respectfully.

"*Sí*. Mama does tend to focus on Cristiano. No question. But you both are her children. She cares equally for you and what happens to you. You're very independent, Rene, and were always different from the beginning," Javier continued, calmly pausing for a moment. "Perhaps she needs to be coming here to the *Iglesia* a little more often to be re-centered. I can remind her of that. She wasn't brought up here like I was, and you… you seem to be drawn here. Perhaps that's God's doing, since that's how you've arrived to us." Javier gently placed his hand on his daughter's hands and gently squeezed them and smiled at her as he finished speaking.

"*Señor* Reyes. I don't mean to interrupt but how exactly did Rene arrive here, if you don't mind sharing with me?" Esther politely interjected after a sense of urgency filled her body.

Javier gave a quick rundown of the events of that day in 1888. Parts that Julia had shared with him and the parts in which he was present regarding Angela, the woman-angel, who delivered Rene.

"*Aye, Dios*. What an event. And what about her name? Was that given by the messenger as well?" Esther asked.

"That was more of Rene's doing perhaps?" Javier spoke with uncertainty at this point.

"She spoke as an infant?" Esther inquired with confusion.

"Well, Julia was asking about the bird we had in the wagon with Rene that night. I had brought her home from a trip just before Rene's messenger arrived at the house. I told her it was a wren. Julia started muttering 'wren' while thinking of a name for the baby, and suddenly, boom, the baby's eyes opened as if she heard her name. It was more strange to Julia since I was busy leading the horses into the night," Javier recalled.

Esther quickly stood as if she were a soldier at attention looking at the door behind Javier and Rene. She looked down at her two *compadres*, her eyes wide, lit with revelation.

"Esther? Are you okay? Is everything okay?" Rene questioned looking back at the door and back at Esther, sliding to the edge of her seat. Her eyes slowly began to glow their vibrant green.

"Come with me. I just remembered something," Esther instructed as she flung her robes around the desk she had been sitting at and quickly headed for the door. Rene and Javier quickly stood and followed Esher out into the hall.

"In the room where I first met Rene, there are secrets of this land that have been guarded over for some centuries. The leaders have not always agreed with them or appreciated them as I've heard, but, regardless, they are here. There are things to know and learn of our lands and communities that have value, and if we are to fully understand and help people, we study it all. But it is in an off limits area so not many clergy members have access to it. As Rene knows… I do," Esther explained as she headed down a spiral flight of stone stairs with Javier and Rene close behind.

Their feet clonked down the stairs in unison, the sound echoing off the walls. Esther pulled out her rosary from her pocket and folded the metal cross in half, and a rigged piece of metal was exposed resembling a key. When Esther inserted the key into the lock, she muttered something under her breath that not even Rene could hear and released the lock.

"The dungeon?" Rene questioned. Her eyes went vibrant green now.

Javier looked at Rene's eyes, feeling slight apprehension, but a feeling of security came over him when Rene touched his sleeved arm.

"This is no dungeon, Rene. Rather a study. Just a little less cared for than I believe it should be. But, it serves its purpose well enough. It's not for everyone, *Mija*." Esther explained, shaking her head in disapproval. She pulled the door open and stepped into the room.

The floor creaked below her feet as they stepped onto the stair landing. Torches suddenly lit around the room along with a single candle at the desk across the room, courtesy of Rene. Esther quickly looked at Rene and Javier, who were unphased by the experience, shook her head in disbelief, and walked down the stairs.

"Perhaps, I'll get familiar with Rene's gifts one day," Esther chuckled to herself carrying her robes down the wooden stairs carefully. She was a small woman, but most women seemed short next to Rene. Esther appeared younger than Javier and handled the stairs with ease. Though she was not an athletic type, she did care for this church and using the stairs seemed to be part of everyday life for her. Caring for her body temple as well as this outer temple was apparent in Esther's godly spirit.

"Now. It is rumored that a river runs under this church. That is why there is no bell in the tower above this area. We will leave it that way for any people outside our group," Esther advised her guests with a nod, and the pair nodded in return." As I shared, not everyone agrees in protecting the stories of this land. Here in this room, we know the truth in history, and Rene found it." She finished as she stood in the middle of the room. The sound of water coming from the small grate in the wall softly echoed against the walls.

Rene's eyes finally mellowed to their usual hazel color and looked over at her father for his thoughts on the room. Javier released a chuckle of curiosity looking up at the ceiling getting distracted by the designs that were now more visible in the center of the room. Javier was a curious type, more so than Rene. His past was even more curious, a mystery his own family still knew little about. Rene often wondered what he was thinking.

"Here," Esther finally instructed as she pointed at the floor nearby. "This is where the dairy is kept." She squatted down and brushed some dust out of a carving in the floor with her thumb with a few flicks of her wrist.

Rene and Javier joined her on their knees, waiting for instruction. Esther inserted her thumb into a keyhole that caused 2 pegs to rise nearby. Esther motioned to them to pull the pegs upward, causing a shelf to suddenly rise up six feet before locking into place with a thud. Rene and Javier scanned over the documents just revealed to them anxiously as their heartbeats slowly increased. They restrained themselves from grabbing anything by placing their hands behind their backs and leaned in with their noses to start reading what they could. Esther quickly glanced over the documents, finding a small book in the middle shelf. Rene and Javier immediately turned their attention to Esther as she carried the book away to the nearby table.

"This is it," Esther whispered urgently as she motioned for Rene and Javier to follow. Rene quickly arrived and sat at the chair Esther motioned at while Javier slowly made his way over. He was still slightly distracted by the other works sitting on the shelves.

"Now. This is in a language you may not be familiar with since it is not so widely spoken here in Puebla, not these days at least. It is Nahuatl," Esther started to explain as Rene quickly chimed in.

"Mama Happy knew Nahuatl," she exclaimed gently as she began to look over the diary. Esther looked at Javier for explanation.
"My grandmother. She was Huastec. My mother keeps her notebooks in hand or around the *posada*, and Rene…" Javier

started motioning at his daughter and the dairy. "...Rene reads." Esther focused on Javier as he continued. "She has accelerated learning abilities. Another gift aside from lighting up a room," Javier lightly joked, nodding at the candle at the table. "It's been a mission of my own to keep her mind positively occupied and educated. Some things, she just seems to know deep down, like she's been here longer than I have..." Javier went on to share with Esther, who nodded in agreement.

"I've been around a long time..." Rene suddenly interjected as she stopped reading and looked up at Esther and Javier before continuing. "This woman. She was the daughter of a chief. When he died, she was sold to the rival tribe by her own mother, so the son of her new husband could take the throne," Rene started to explain.

"*Sí, Mija*, women have not been as highly regarded as they should be by people, or men for that matter. Pardon me, *Señor* Reyes..." Esther interrupted apologetically looking at Javier who shook his head in agreement and sighed in disappointment.

"The other tribe used her as a slave, caring for homes and ... other improper things," Rene continued quietly with a sniffle as she looked over the handwriting before her. She took a deep breath and continued, as Javier placed his hands on her shoulder to comfort her. Rene began to paraphrase the story before her for Esther and her father.

"But she did find love. A young man she helped care for in his mother's house. There was a secret marriage between the two. She was only my age. They were going to meet one night when he became fully well and started to work so they could move away... She waited for him by the river, pregnant, but he never came. She later found out that his mother poisoned him for marrying outside the tribe, but she didn't know about the baby growing inside her servant, her grandchild. That was their secret. She wore large dresses to cover her belly… She was so sad that night waiting for him, there with a basket of supplies for their escape." Rene closed her eyes and was no longer reading the dairy in front of her. Leaving her hands on the table, she faced her palms upward as if to receive something.

"A daughter was born, and this woman was afraid. She could not imagine raising this baby alone, as she was a slave. She dumped out a sack of fruits she had packed into the water. She wrapped the baby in a piece of cloth from her own large dress and placed her into the sack… she kissed and whispered goodbye to the baby and tied the top closed. The supplies in the basket were emptied into the river too, and she put clay around the bottom to seal up the holes. The sack holding the baby was gently placed into a basket. She waded into the water to cast off the basket, and I floated away into the mist…" Rene whispered with a sniffle.

"I?" Javier whispered looking at Esther, who shook her head, pointing back at Rene.

"The basket disappeared into the mist, and a gust of wind blew suddenly... there was a cry from the baby. The woman ran out into the river to help but, when she found the basket, the baby and the cloth in the tied sack were gone. She had named her *Occeppa tlacati*, meaning born again, also known as Rene." Rene finished speaking and opened her eyes, blinking rapidly before looking over at her father.

"*Sí*, Rene. *La Dona Marina,* or some call *La Malinche*, had a child before the two we have heard of existing already," Esther added. "Sometimes we can be quick to blame people for the things they've done, but we don't realize what they've gone through to become that way first. That's part of healing a mind too. Acknowledging the past." Esther looked down at Rene and placed her hand on her shoulder.

"We know her story. But yes, not always the whole story... till now," Javier said heavily.

After closing up the study and returning to the main hall, the three of them said their goodbyes and began the rest of their day. They agreed they would return regularly to discuss their findings and help Rene with any concerns she may have.

On the outside, Rene seemed calm and collected, while her mind swirled with thoughts. One in particular was the meaning of her native outfits she would wear in her dreams was now explained. She was the granddaughter of a chief. As she would see in local artwork, those headdresses were usually only worn by a chief and she wondered why she wore one in her dream realm. That finally made sense, and that was comforting to her. Javier walked in silence with Rene, processing things in his own mind, as they made their way to the gift shop. He thought about how Rene may be feeling too but patiently waited in hopes she would speak first, but it never happened. As they arrived at the shop door, Rene stopped suddenly and turned to her father.

"I'll find a way to tell Mama what I can. If I can't, I'll tell her to ask you. Okay, *Papi*?" Rene instructed, looking into her father's eyes boldly.

"That will do, Rene. I'll have your back." Javier agreed as he opened the door for his daughter to enter before parting his own way.

Inside the shop, Julia was behind the counter with Ernestina, Cristiano, and Alana. Ernestina and Alana's stay had not been decided as of yet how long it would be. She had been experiencing her own troubles at home with her husband, and her parents were unfortunately not of much help. She was becoming estranged slowly from having a close relationship with them like her older sister Julia. Since Julia could use the help and Nina needed the work, they were happy to let them stay. Julia missed her anyway; having the help was a plus.

"Good morning Nina, Good morning, Mama," Rene greeted her family when she entered the shop door. As the bell rang, the two had looked up and saw Rene and smiled. Cristiano and Alana then ran to the front door to see her.
"Rene, can we go play with you outside?" Alana and Cristiano asked excitedly in unison.

"Yeah, we want to go to the river!" Cristiano demanded with a smile.

Rene smiled and laughed as each of her hands and arms were pulled on by the two kids. Alana stopped and touched some marks on Rene's hands, catching her mother's attention.

"Yes, Rene, would you mind taking them? Nina and I will be here. We can handle this, *Amor*." Julia pleaded with Rene as she hustled around the store restocking shelves from the *Dia de los Muertos* sales.

"Okay, *Mama*. Let's go amigos!" Rene ordered the kids excitedly as she opened the door ahead of the kids. She waved bye to her Nina, who watched them exit the store.

"Did you see that Julia?" Ernestina quickly asked her big sister as the door shut.

"What's that Rebekita?" Julia replied back instinctively, still preoccupied with some boxes to unpack. Rebecca was Ernestina's middle name, and Julia had her own nickname for her little sister.
"Rene's hand. Alana saw some scratches on her hand, and I saw her touch them. What happened? Was she in a fight?" Ernestina inquired suspiciously.

"Rene in a fight? What?" Julia gasped, finally looking more attentive as her face became filled with a look of dread.

"Aye Julia, I don't know what happened. Relax. You just need to ask her later. I'm just telling you we saw some scratches or something, and I'm asking what happened. Breathe." Ernestina replied, trying to calm her sister.

"Oh. Okay. *Aye, Dios*. I get so busy with things that I forget to check in with Rene. She keeps things to herself, and I'm not sure why." Julia muttered as she moved around the store and began to make a large pot of coffee at the small stove.

"Well, I think I know why…" Ernestina coughed with a tone of insinuation as she arranged items on a table.

"What?" Julia barked, looking over at her sister as she made her way over to her.

"You know *what*, *Hermana*. You get stressed. Maybe it's because you're the oldest, or you were raised by the *abuelos* in such serenity that this world triggers you so easily. I know I'm young, but I do know some things, and I know about the stress of relationships, parenting, and family. Especially our family." Ernestina added with a chuckle, nudging her sister as she turned to look out the front window into the plaza.

"I hope I'm not hurting Rene. I want her to tell me things! I love her," Julia whispered with a sigh.

"We never want to hurt our kids. The sooner we learn this about ourselves, the sooner we can fix it. Right?" Ernestina finished, looking back at Julia with a smile. Julia cracked a small smile in return and nodded in agreement.

"Well, I didn't want to go home yet," Cristiano whined as Rene and the kids walked up the road to the *posada*.

"BUT, I'M TIRED. AND HUNGRY," Alana whined back.

"Okay, Okay, you two. There will be other days to explore by the river and hike… And Cris, Alana isn't used to all this outdoor stuff living over in the big city, so be nice," Rene reminded her brother as he ran ahead of them. She then looked down at her little cousin with a patient smile.

Looking back up the road towards the *posada* past Cristiano, she saw someone exiting the front door looking in her direction. Rene sensed a nervousness coming from the young man's direction as he began looking around and fixing his hair. Confirmed by his frantic glances off the side of the road, it was as if he were looking for a way to escape. Rene and Alana picked up the pace for the final stretch home. As Rene got closer to the stranger, her mind raced trying to remember if she'd seen him before when an image from the party popped up. It was the boy named Carlos, Ana said, and he had almost crashed into her last night.

"Who are you?" Cris demanded with a stomp in front of Carlos, putting his hands on his hips.

"Cristiano. We don't talk to people like that, remember?" Rene corrected her brother, smacking him gently on the shoulder with the back of her hand before Carlos could answer.

"I'm sorry about that, Carlos," Rene apologized, as Cristiano huffed and ran off to the *posada*.

"Wait…how did you…?" Carlos asked in confusion.
"You worked at the party last night, right?" Rene inquired, already knowing the answer but was trying to open up conversation for Carlos, who seemed a little tongue tied.

"Yeah. Right. Sorry again I almost crashed into you, Rene. I just came by to return the suit your father lent me," Carlos stammered, as he patted down the back of his hair, still trying to make himself look more put together.

"I see. Well, no worries. Everything worked out, Carlos," Rene said with a smile, as she began walking towards the house again. Carlos just kept his eyes on her as she started walking away. Alana, who had been standing next to Rene just looking at the two talking about last night, chimed in next to Rene.

"I wish I could've stayed up all night!" Alana shared sweetly, thinking about the party herself now.

"When you're fifteen, maybe you will!" Rene laughed. She patted her cousin on the head gently as they walked on.

"You can call me Charlie!" Carlos quickly added, as Rene walked on trying to get her attention one last time. He was still standing in place where Cristiano had stopped him.

"Okay, Charlie," she called back and waved at Charlie. As she spun around still keeping in motion towards the *posada*, Alana did her best to mimic Rene's spin and wave with a giggle.

"Tell your uncle thanks for the haircut too! I forgot!" He called out once more, cupping his mouth.

Rene saluted him in acknowledgment, still facing the *posada*.

Carlos stood there a moment, watching her make her way home before realizing he was staring. He shook his head quickly, awkwardly looking around to see if anyone noticed, and ran off towards the village.

Chapter 9
Soul Cry

Rene's "15th" year flew by quickly. Over the past year, things even got better between her and her mother. It was only a few months after her first fight with the demon woman that Rene was able to tell her mother, finally expressing what she had been going through. The wisdom that Ernestina had shared with her big sister had also sunk in and opened up Julia's heart and mindset towards her daughter.

The deep fears and concerns that filled Julia's heart were pouring out and affecting her daughter's ability to share her own troubles with her. Julia had to put aside her negative-seeming reactions in order to be available to Rene if she wanted her to be open with her. That moment came for Julia and Rene over *Candelaria*, just after having a candle blessed at the *Catedral* where Esther served and Rene now studied privately below it. After learning her own history and even the history of the people of this realm, this mend in their relationship was much needed for Rene.

The months that followed were even more crucial for Rene's development, especially mentally and emotionally. Rene always had this divine peace over her mind and emotions up to this point in her life, unlike her mother. Having an inner peace no one could explain was a gift imparted to her too. However, she also wanted to share with others in order to better process and learn what her next move would be. On top of everything in her family, life, and work, she was studying human behaviors and psychology too. Since "healing the mind" had become a mission weighing heavy on her heart, it had also become a passion. Esther assisted in part of her education from a faith standpoint often, as she also considered remedies that entered her mind divinely.

     Rene found herself waking up early more these days like her father and usually enjoying coffee with her Nana. Afterwards, she would make her way to the *Catedral* to study before helping her mom at the shop, carrying both a Bible and a psychology book that Dr. Rameriz had given her. Rene considered that if Dr. Rameriz could help heal a body, she had maybe learned about healing a mind too. She was right. Rene found out that Doctor Rameriez had sat in on a few lectures while in medical school in New York that discussed psychology, or 'alienation', she mentioned they also called it. It was one of those rare times Dr. Rameriz was at home being just "Mama" when Rene asked her about it. She then went to a trunk she kept in the common room of the house and pulled out a few books she had acquired about hysteria and other theories on mental health and generously gave them to Rene. Receiving these books had Rene feeling like she just received the family's fortune, but of course the Lombardi sisters had no interest in being doctors– ever.

Rene studied them feverishly, and even though her powers of accelerated learning retained the information, she carried those books, along with her book of prayers as if they were her own comfort blankets. In her mind, she felt like it was as though the words would seep out of the book covers and soak into her very skin, and the words would flow through her veins and fill her mind.

Cristiano had a comfort item too, a pillow he would carry around at home. It seemed as if they were attached at the hip. Anytime he tried taking that pillow out in public with him, he was reminded to put it back by his mother or father. He didn't seem to require it when Rene was with him, but the rest of the family always thought he was up to something suspicious with that pillow as if he was usually using it for more than comfort, but also protection. His parents suspected he was up to something reckless, but that would not be the case, they would later on find out.

Rene eventually shared that she would like to go to the University of Padua, where Mr. Lambardi's father taught as a professor back in Italy. Rene's study habits eventually made an impression on Ana's father, and he'd mentioned what Grandpa Lombardi did back home. With that connection, Rene would surely be able to study there in time she had hoped and she eventually brought it up to her parents. Hesitant at first, her parents eventually agreed that since Javier had made contacts in Italy as well, they would do their part to see this happen for their daughter. She had gifts and abilities that didn't need to be confined to Puebla but could be shared around the world. They would start making arrangements to meet the Lombardis in Italy that summer on their next trip overseas to import goods. Italy was a land close to Javier's soul, as he'd traveled there often before the kids came into the picture.

In the early summer, Julia and Javier traveled to Italy with Gilberto to meet the Lombardi family. His passage back home was a gift from the Reyes family, as he assisted in getting this formal education for Rene. He had not been back to Italy to see his family in years, and the Reyes family also agreed that they would need a guide since Javier had never been in the northern territory much before. Little Cristiana also went along on the journey, since Doctor Rameriz would be left behind to manage the office and two older girls.

Back in Puebla, Rene was put in charge of managing Cristiano, mainly since their parents would be gone a while. Nana would be managing the *posada* along with Uncle Tomás, who had also started to pick up an internship with a local barber in the town to learn further how to cut hair. Ever since he had cut Charlie's hair for the party, he finally considered it for more than just a hobby. He was good at it, creative even. Maria was not thrilled at the thought of her son's new profession, but Tomás never seemed content working in any of the other family businesses.

There wasn't a high demand or need for more barbers in the town, but Tomás was steadfast in pursuing this path, regardless of his mother's silent– and not so silent– protests. Javier was supportive, however, and that's all Tomas needed in order for him to keep going. Besides, he had cut Javier's hair for years now, and Charlie was pleased with his own haircut too. Rene requested her hair also be cut short, but given her growing athletic physique, she thought twice about it and decided to keep a more feminine look, even if it was just long hair. Ana agreed with her, as she had always coveted Rene's long hair over her unruly poof of curls on her head.

  That summer, Rene made time to also teach Cristiano self-defense. He admitted to being teased by the other kids in town about having a glass eye, and since the color did not match his natural eye color exactly, it was noticeable. Concerned for her brother's safety and possibly against her mother's wishes, since she never asked for permission, she taught Cristiano moves of her ancestors. Some things Javier had taught her, but others she had learned in her studies and, of course, in her dream realm. Rene knew she wouldn't always be at her brother's side to protect him, but he could learn to protect himself mentally and physically. She reminded him of his value to their family and friends that mattered and how he was valued by God himself. She let him know that *"sticks and stones may break your bones, but words can't hurt you,"* so long as he chose not to believe the lies from those who taunted him. Cristiano once questioned Rene's eye color that summer, noting that no one in the whole family had green in their eyes except for Rene. Ana had the fairer eyes so he wondered if maybe they really were sisters, since they would joke about it. She teased back "Yes, I am a Lombardi, but your family needed me, so here I am!" and then distracted him with a tickle attack that led to a wrestling match. She was off the hook, for now at least.

Rene was concerned for her brother and what he may experience as he grew older and being looked at differently because of his eye. However, so long as he stayed focused on all he could do instead of what he couldn't, he would be ok. She was going to stay focused on that too for his upbringing and hoped that not every person he'd meet would judge him by his appearance. Rene eventually found the axolotl with the injury at the river again one day and told Cristiano about how it seemed to have healed itself since it certainly had the designs and markings of the one she had seen the summer before.

"Maybe my eye will grow back too!" Cristiano declared with hope.

"We'll see what God says, *Hermano*. You're smart, and you like making things. Maybe you'll invent something!" Rene replied, giving Cristiano encouragement towards his thoughts.

"Yes! Maybe!" Cristiano exclaimed, as his mind immediately seemed to go to work. He also spent some time trying to catch the little creature to keep as a pet, but its slippery body just seemed to get away with ease. Mama Happy's book mentioned that these were strange creatures that seemed to "shape shift" overtime, growing limbs and missing body parts they'd lost. This was written next to the recipe that spoke about cooking them for dinner too. Yuck.

Meanwhile, Rene's and Ana's friendship continued to grow. They would still spend time together when they weren't working with their parents or learning at home. Ana continued to show a talent for the arts and studied with Julia at times. However, the lack of faith Ana had in herself as an artist and the safety of the known family business doing clerical work for her mother held her back. After all, she was the one who painted the mural on the stair landing for Rene's party and even helped paint designs on the dinnerware, Julia believed in her talent too. However, Ana was also constantly getting distracted by the opposite sex. Getting into a relationship and getting married one day seemed to be at the front of her mind. Marrying young was the norm, afterall, and she would not be left out. Even Lidi had started dating lately. As shy as she was, she found someone equally awkward, and it was working out. Ana, however, seemed to be in a rush and didn't put too much thought into her relationship choices other than his looks and whether or not he had a job. Personality or character traits were not paid attention to, and that led to toxic relationships for Ana.

Rene, on the other hand, was always focused on learning. Sure, she'd look on when Ana pointed someone out, gawking at their looks. However, knowing she had plans to leave Mexico to study one day, the thought of leaving a partner behind would not be something she wanted on her plate. Saying goodbye to her family and Ana would be hard enough.

Plus, there were the demons.

Rene fought the demons in her dream realm regularly. Sometimes they'd even get away from her before finishing them off, and this concerned her. Would they be back, or would they come to her reality like they did after her *quinceñera*? She would soon find out.

November 1, 1899

"Rene, Ana is here!" Julia called out to Rene as Ana entered the *posada's* lobby. As she turned towards the hall, there was Rene behind her giving her a startle. "Oh, *Mija* I didn't see you!" Julia exclaimed. "You scared me!" Julia laughed nervously holding her chest.

"Sorry, Mama." Rene quietly chuckled apologetically, hugging her mother gently. When she pulled away, Julia looked her daughter over, head to toe, to see what she was wearing. She smiled as her eyes noted the winged charm on her neck. Rene had worn it everyday since her birthday last year. Rene smiled back at her mother just as Julia started up.

"Ana, Rene needs some festivity here don't you think?" Julia asked Ana motioning at Rene's face with her head cocked to the side. Rene's heart sank, and she closed her eyes. She had put on a blouse, skirt, and her sash to hopefully appease her mother enough. She didn't want to hear this comment.

Ana nodded feverishly in agreement at Julia and let out a squeal. She had painted her own face for the fiesta and would love to have Rene do the same.

"Stop by the shop and use my paints, Ana." Julia added looking over at Ana and back at Rene. "It's your birthday, Rene. Let's have some fun! Don't be a lazy woman. Own it!" Julia finished enthusiastically.

Rene let out a sigh as her shoulders sank. Julia's face grew annoyed for a moment, but Rene suddenly shook it off, smiled, nodded at her mother, and kissed her on the cheek goodbye. As the girls exited the *posada* stepping into the sunset, Julia noticed Rene's boots under her skirt and shook her head in disapproval. She let out a scoff, throwing her hands in the air and made her way towards the kitchen.

There was a *fiesta* that night at the town square, just as there was every year for *Dia de los Muertos*. Rene and Ana were allowed to attend as long as they stayed together as a chaperone to each other. It was a fair request they never seemed to argue with when there was an event in town. They appreciated the independence their parents gave them.

As the girls walked down the road to the plaza and the cemetery in the distance was in sight, Ana quieted down from her chatty self and nervously looked over at Rene.

"Getting any weird feelings, Ren?" Ana half joked, her voice almost down to a whisper.

"Weird feelings? Did I tell you I get 'weird' feelings?" Rene laughed loudly. Ana laughed back nervously but quickly interjected in a serious tone.
"Ren! For Real!" Ana whined, shoving Rene to the side of the road towards the bushes that surrounded the perimeter as they walked past the cemetery.

"You're ok, Ana! I'm here. The bodyguard!" Rene said in a deep tone voice putting her fists on her hips standing still like a statue for a moment looking into the distance. Ana rolled her eyes and kept walking.

"Okay! I'm just kidding around Ana!" Rene hollered as she jogged to catch up with her. "But really I don't want you to worry. I deal with this 'stuff' all the time. Sometimes, I don't feel like I sleep at night!" Rene assured Ana, putting her hand on her shoulder. Ana sighed in response as she relaxed. "No weird feelings though, seriously!" Rene added with a smile. The two quietly walked past the cemetery before Rene broke the silence again as they reached the plaza.

"But demons can be anywhere, not just cemeteries, *amiga*." Rene said under her breath, clenching her teeth into a fake grin as they arrived at the town square's edge when their group of friends started approaching them.

These friends were mostly Ana's since she met so many of them at the Doctor's office, but Rene joined in on the group chats pretty well. She was a good listener, and most people appreciated that. Not long after arriving, off in the distance, Charlie caught Rene's eye as she moved through the crowd with Ana and her entourage. Charlie eventually saw Rene and waved with a smile as he stood in his work apron near a friend he had been talking to. He was apparently working at his aunt's food stand for the town celebration. Rene smiled and waved back just as Ana grabbed her hand, quickly jerking her arm downwards.

"Oh my God, there he is!" Ana angrily whispered under her breath as she squeezed Rene's hand.

"What? Who?" Rene answered with a slight scowl on her face, pulling her hand away and adjusting her blouse around her neck.

"Jorge! Who else?" He's here with Angelica!" Ana grunted annoyedly back at Rene.

"Easy!" Rene whispered back, curling her lip upward in anger. "I can't keep track," she added under her breath.

"What was that?" Ana shot back looking at Rene with a side eye.

"Oh, I see him. Well, shoot, I'm sorry, Ana," Rene replied as nicely as possible to support her friend's emotional state. Jorge was touching the side of Angelica's arm gently before putting his arm around her waist and led her into the crowd out of sight. Ana was caught in a trance like stare watching the two being flirty with each other.

"I can't… I gotta go… We need to go." Ana stammered as tears welled up in her eyes. Rene looked over at Ana as she turned her face away from the crowd, and her feet followed quickly in the direction of her view to scuttle away.

"Nature calls…" Rene impulsively told a friend nearby. "We'll be back soon." She chuckled nervously as she quickly followed after Ana.

Rene stomped up to Ana in her boots and grabbed her arm. Ana's clouded mind caused her to wonder in which direction to walk in like she was lost. Rene helped direct her steps before a man on a horse knocked her over in the poorly lit street.

"Okay, this way Ana. Time to go to the shop." Rene instructed her emotional friend, who was full-on crying now.

As Rene led Ana to the shop, she began whining through her sobs about Jorge, recalling memories and the hopes she had for their future. Rene just listened and kept affirming her friends complaints and agreeing with her, for the most part, so Ana would feel heard and supported.

As they arrived at the shop, Ana had started to slow her crying and was silent now, aside from the sniffling and choppy breaths left behind from the crying. Rene opened the door to the dark shop and led Ana inside who took her time getting through the threshold, dragging her feet in depression. Rene let out an impatient sigh as she finally closed the door behind them, but not before a cold draft made its way inside too.

"Ahh!" Ana screamed jumping behind Rene.

"What?" Rene shouted, as a single candle then lit by the counter.

"Jeez. I forgot about that armor your papa has here!" Ana recalled, as she put her hand over her heart letting out a sigh of relief.

"Ugh. You're like my mama now, Ana." Rene replied, annoyed, taking a deep breath as she walked away from the front door.

"Well, that'll make a girl stop crying…" Ana continued nonchalantly as she walked towards the counter.
"Nice! So now we don't need to paint my face. Let's go!" Rene quipped as she glanced at the armor's red face mask before looking at Ana with a grin. She started to turn towards the door in slow motion to leave when she sensed a faint presence growing inside the shop. She paused for a moment in thought but shrugged it off since it wasn't strong enough to get worked up about.

"No! I'm fixing my face, and I'm doing yours! Please?" Ana quickly replied in desperation. "Come on, I need this Ren. You know this makes me happy. You're the one who told me to keep my hobbies!" Ana added with a grin with her hands on her hips.

"Okay, Okay. I know. I know." Rene grumbled with a half smile as she stomped towards the back of the shop. Something triggered in the back of her mind again as that faint presence started feeling stronger and now unfriendly. She remained collected so Ana wouldn't know something was up after being so emotional and just finally calming down.

After what seemed like hours to Rene but only minutes to Ana, Rene's face was completely painted. Ana had gone back and forth in conversation with Rene about Jorge. Rene reminded Ana to leave Angelica out of the topic because Jorge was a problem in himself. He seemed to be a ladie's man in the first place, and that's what sucked Ana in. Ana whined, but Rene spent her side of the conversation trying to build up her friend and her worthiness of a good and healthy relationship one day. On the inside, she was trying to figure out what this strange presence that she felt inside the shop.

"One day, one day, one day," Ana mocked in a whiney voice as she cleaned up Julia's paints and put them away.
Rene got up from her chair and ignored Ana's impatience as she went to one of the back storage closets to look in the mirror. If Rene's face were not already completely painted in multi-colored designs, it would have turned white in shock.

"It's beautiful, right?" Ana beamed in the mirror's reflection next to Rene's.

Rene stood there in the closet in her bloomers feeling a little too vulnerable for once in her life, taking a deep breath before replying.

"Yes… you're a great artist, Ana. No one will recognize me, but it's great," Rene replied back as nicely as possible, smiling in the mirror's reflection looking at Ana.

"Okay! Let's go back to the party. Forget Jorge. There's plenty of fish in the sea, and I am a fisher of men!" Ana said confidently with a laugh, placing the paints back in the storage closet next to Rene. Annoyed, Rene refrained from rubbing her forehead in frustration in response to Ana's comment.

"Yeah! Go. I'm gonna put my skirt back on, lock up, and I'll be right there!" Rene replied eagerly, needing a minute to herself to decompress. She had a multitude of feelings she was now experiencing because of her decorated face, her friend's erratic emotions, and, of course, the strange presence still in the room.

"Okay!" Ana shouted as she happily jumped to face the door, adjusted her top and skirt, took a deep breath, and headed out the front door as Rene waved her off. As the door opened and shut, another gush of cold air rushed into the shop, causing the armor to rattle.

Strange. Rene thought, glancing at the armor suspiciously.

She looked at the armor a while feeling her body temperature rise slightly. She looked over the details of the large Samurai suit before her and wondered why someone gave that to her father in the first place. It was something she usually pondered while looking at it when she was working in the shop. Javier traveled the world and brought home many things. Julia, being somewhat submissive, especially in the early years of their marriage, never interrogated him about it. Rene wondered why she never bothered asking him about it before either.

Refocusing on the events at hand and getting back to the party, Rene turned away from the suit and walked to the back of the store. She entered the storage room and put the mirror back in its place and proceeded to put her skirt and sash back on. As she turned her back to the door and picked up her skirt, she heard a low sound of a grunt followed by metal ringing. Instinctively, she dropped her garment and grabbed another other sword her father owned from a display shelf in the closet where she stood.

One hand on the sheath and the other on the grip ready to draw the blade, she slowly turned around, dropping to a knee drawing the sword back. No one was there to be seen, but that unfriendly presence she felt earlier was even stronger now. Holding her position on the floor ready to jab, her eyes turned green, and the hairs on her neck and arms stood in attention. She waited there in anticipation of what was coming next. In the front room to her left, another sound arose. Though it was still faint even with her keen hearing, she knew something was there. A few seconds later, the sound of gentle footsteps slowly approached her direction, and that sound of ringing metal filled her ears again. She rose up slightly from her knee but remained low to the ground. Gripping her sword tighter in her right hand, she picked up her sash from the shelf with the other. Something inside her seemed to alert her of its necessity for what was coming next.

The footsteps stopped a moment and then *WHOOSH* a dark figure dashed down the hall before she could attack. Rene popped up and out of the storage room in time to see the Samurai armor shoulder check the back door and break free into the alley.

Oh no… Rene thought to herself quickly as she ran after it into the night.

Rene chased the possessed armor through the back streets of the city in what seemed to be heading in the direction of the cemetery. As she caught up to the stealthy demon, she whipped her sash around its neck like lassoing a calf. As she pulled it down backwards onto its back, the Samurai somersaulted backwards instantly and flipped into a standing position. It quickly swung its sword across Rene's body, clipping parts of her blouse with the tip of the blade as Rene jumped backwards, escaping any real injury.

How will I get that thing out of there!? She questioned herself. *No way that armor has been possessed all this time.*

The two continued fighting in the dim empty streets as the Samurai kept heading in the direction of the cemetery. Rene calculated her way out of this scenario in her mind as she also began praying no one would be around the cemetery to witness this event or become injured along the way. She was thankful again for this new face art she wore for the moment. She would at least be unrecognizable to avoid awkward questions later. At least, that is what she told herself as she chased after the Samurai. They had passed a few *borrachos* along the way sleeping against the back of the buildings with their faces buried into their belongings.

As they reached the outskirts of the cemetery, something told her to not let this monster enter the gates. She recalled similar situations she experienced in her dreams and sought the wisdom in her mind of things to do to end this fight. The two continued to fight in circular motion. She had the suit focused on her and not the cemetery for now. Her necklace had been swinging around her neck as she fought the samurai and took a moment to still it. Upon touching it, an evasion maneuver quickly entered her mind just as the armor thrusted forward with its sword at Rene.

SWOOSH She jumped on top of the samurai's sword quickly as it came at her and cartwheeled off his helmet, taking her ten feet away from the monster in the armor now. Upon landing, she dropped her sword and sheath to the floor and charged at the demon, exploding from the ground from her hands and feet like a rocket from a launch pad. As her opponent clumsily swung its sword again, she dodged it with a side flip over its shoulder. As she landed directly behind it, she quickly jammed her hand in the gap between the chest gear and facemask of the demon and slammed it down backwards towards the ground again. This time, the back of the helmet collided with a large boulder, detaching the head from the bodysuit and rolled away in the bushes at the cemetery perimeter. As Rene continued to push the suit further down forcefully till it hit the ground and put her knee on its chest. Then, an evil soul cry escaped into the air, and a cloud of dust exploded from the suit. Rene turned her face away to shield her eyes from the dust when a menacing laugh filled the air. The sound strangely echoed in the trees above as if it were perched to rest there. Rene let go of the suit, quickly stood, and looked up into the trees in concern, but nothing was there to be seen.

"*Papi*, I don't think this isn't over," She said out loud with a heavy sigh, looking back down the suit, shaking her head in disapproval. As she knelt back down beside the lifeless armor, she knew deep down that this demon would certainly return again.

As Rene gathered the armor, helmet, and weapons in hand, her necklace caught onto part of the suit. While she was busy heaving the suit into her arms, it broke free from her neck without her noticing and clung to the armor a moment. Once more, Rene adjusted the armor and accessories in her grip before making her way towards the backstreets to the shop. The charm finally released from the suit and fell to the ground outside the cemetery property. Preoccupied with getting out of possible public view, again, Rene didn't sense its absence.

Maybe I should just bury this armor in the woods somewhere? Rene considered as she began hauling her father's giant armor keepsake back to the shop.

Chapter 10
Charlie

Rene was left with an uneasy feeling thinking about the eerie laugh that lingered in the trees, uncertain what would happen next. After returning the armor and making sure the shop was back to normal, she returned to the plaza for the festivities. Shortly after arriving, she found Ana already chatting and giggling away with a new guy. Just as Rene rolled her eyes and stepped back to turn in the opposite direction, dragging her floppy skirt with her, there was Charlie. Rene nearly collided heads with him as she was looking down to make sure her skirt completed the turn as he was about to tap her on the shoulder to say hi.

"Oh shoot, sorry!" Rene apologized, as she had felt she was skimming someone's face with her hair, causing Charlie to step back quickly, bumping into another person in the crowd. "Oh. Charlie. Hi!" Rene added with a friendly smile once she saw who it was.

"Sorry about that," Charlie quickly apologized to the guy behind him before turning back towards Rene. "Rene, Hi. Oh yea, I'm fine thanks," Charlie responded awkwardly. He shook his head realizing he hadn't been asked anything.

"Is this going to be a yearly thing bumping into you or something?" Rene joked with a chuckle, recalling the vision of almost crashing into his tray of food at her party through her photographic memory.

Charlie tilted his head upward in thought for a moment.

"My party last year. I really was hoping food fell all over that dress so I could change. These things are NOT my thing!" Rene laughed as she hauled her skirt off the ground a few inches and let it fall back down over her boots. Charlie laughed, remembering their encounter at the quinceañera.

"That's right!" Charlie laughed, as he smacked his hand into his forehead. Noticing sweat on his brow maybe from working or maybe from nervousness, he quickly wiped it off. "Well, happy birthday then too," Charlie quickly added with a smile.

"Thank you, I can't believe you even recognized me in this war paint Ana put on me," Rene joked back motioning at her face with a laugh. Charlie held in his laugh, closed his eyes, and shook his head with a smile. Rene casually looked over the crowd around them before looking back at Charlie again.

"I thought it was a bird face?" Charlie questioned cautiously.

"It is! But still, I think she got carried away. 'Lost in the art,' she calls it," Rene mimicked Ana in a high pitched voice and a chuckle. "Anyway, it's a lot of paint. Where's yours?" Rene asked Charlie, motioning at his face.

"Oh, I…" Charlie started to say, as Rene started looking around the crowd again, this time with a hint of concern as she scrunched her eyebrows in thought. Charlie looked around, wondering what she was looking for as his confidence waned.

Rene looked back at Charlie to finish his sentence, raising her eyebrows as she smiled.

"I'm just kidding. No one wants a clown face like this. I didn't," She whispered with a laugh. "Are you working tonight? I saw you over there with your aunt?" Rene asked motioning towards their grill setup.

"Aunts. Yea. They gave me a break to come visit with everyone. It's a busy night," Charlie answered, looking over at his family in the distance and then back at Rene. "You'd think with there being so many of them, they'd not need me." Charlie shrugged with a sigh, staring down at Rene. He was just slightly taller than she.

"How many do you have?" Rene laughed looking in their direction again.

"Let's just say more aunts than you'll find at a picnic," Charlie heaved, rolling his eyes with a smirk.

"Gotcha," Rene laughed. "Well it's nice to have family nearby. To me, anyways, mine is kinda spread out. But at least I have Ana and her family. They're like my second family at this point." Rene finished sharing just as Lidi abruptly walked up to her and Charlie.

"Ren, where is Ana?" Lidi quickly blurted out.

"She was right there by the fountain with some guy talking a few minutes ago…" Rene quickly answered, stepping on her tippy toes looking for Ana. Charlie started looking around for Ana, scanning the crowd as well. Rene sighed with a grunt when Ana

139

was nowhere to be seen. "Great. OK, I'll go look for her," Rene informed Lidi.

"Okay… and what happened to your blouse?" Lidi quickly added motioning at her top. Rene looked down at her top just then, noticing some cuts from her battle with the Samurai earlier.

"Uhh. There was a cat… I gotta go. See you later Charlie," Rene lied, grinning with embarrassment. With one hand, she grabbed her shirt near her stomach where a large hole was, and her skirt with the other hand and ran off into the crowd.

"Bye, Rene," Charlie faintly added in disappointment as Rene stormed off.

Charlie spent a few more moments in the heart of the party when he found a couple of friends and shared greetings with them. One of them had noticed Charlie talking to Rene earlier and asked if they had got a chance to dance. In frustration, Charlie responded with a "no luck and no time" excuse and shrugged. After a while, his friends eventually ventured off to further mingle in the crowds and meet up with some girls to talk to and hopefully dance with.

Charlie, on the other hand, needed to get back to his Aunt's food stand. Just as soon as he arrived, one of the Figeroa sisters handed their nephew an apron and the grill spatula to get back to cooking. Charlie was a hard worker, and he had respect for his aunts and their drive to serve others through this business. He did his best to be an extension of that same energy when it came to serving the customers. Throughout the night, a couple of patrons mentioned how he was starting to look more like his father but had his mother's smile. Unsure of who they were, his aunts told him they were old friends that had known his parents there in

Puebla. Charlie's thoughts then drifted towards his parents, and he became distracted. He looked down at the little gold ring on his left pinky finger and gave it a few turns with his thumb and pointer finger of his right hand. His mood was now going further south than it had gone once Rene had run off to look for Ana. His Aunt Olivia noticed sadness now overcoming Charlie's face. She knew how much Charlie thought of his parents and missed his mother.

"*Mijo*, I think we can take it from here for a while, why don't you go take these pans to the house and come back later for clean up?" *Tia* Olivia, suggested handing some large pans to Charlie, taking his mind off the little gold ring he was playing with. Charlie nodded, taking the pans from his aunt, and walked off into the night towards home.

After arriving back at their house and leaving the pans in the kitchen, Charlie noticed light coming from one of his aunt's bedroom doors. He carefully cracked the door further open, as he did not usually go snooping around in his aunts' bedroom. When he peered inside, he saw that there was a candle left lit on a side table filled with pictures. He gently stepped in the room to get a closer look at the photos. Some faces he knew, and some he didn't. As he looked them over, there in the back was a picture of his mother. He carefully picked up the photo to look at it closer.

His eyes began to well up with tears as he looked at his mother, gently smiling back at him holding his little brother, who was sleeping in her arms. The picture was one of the last she had taken of her before she was taken from this world. Now Charlie was missing her even more that night, and he didn't need a special holiday to remind him of her. His daily reminder was her ring he wore everyday on his pinky finger that he was playing with earlier. His Father had given it to him after she passed away, too heartbroken to keep it for himself. He'd given it to him before he left to America to find migrant farm work not long after burying her there in town, leaving Charlie and Diego to be raised by his wife's sisters. Charlie's father, also named Carlos, was suffering with such depression he felt unfit to care for his sons. He had also grown up as an orphan and did not have any other family of his own to his knowledge to help him with the boys. Carlos would send money down along with an update of where he would be staying for the time being every month to the aunts to help support Charlie and Diego over the years. Staying in Puebla caused him so much pain having all those memories he shared with Charlie's mom and his lonely childhood, so he stayed away from there now.

Charlie put down the photograph, blew out the candle, and left his Aunt's room, closing the door behind him. As he made his way back towards the front of the dimly lit house, he heard mumbling coming from the empty kitchen table. He carefully approached the table draped with different cloths and squatted beside it. As he lifted the hanging cloth, he found Diego asleep in a fort he made underneath the wooden table. He was dreaming of something apparently. Charlie felt like he was kind of a father to Diego with theirs being gone, he cared for him extra carefully whenever he could. Diego was less than a year old when their mother died, so he didn't share in Charlie or his father's pain of her passing much. Besides, he had his aunt's love, as did Charlie, but that was enough for Diego. Charlie gently dragged his little brother out from the fort on the blanket he had been lying on, picked him up, and carried him off to bed.

Little Diego was lighter than the swine his aunts had him haul around for their cooking business, which aided in developing Charlie's strength. He had also started taking an interest in the new rising sport of boxing in Mexico, so that kept him athletic.

Not to mention, the aunts made sure he was never hungry with all the food they cooked for their business, giving him an overall full and muscular physique. "I'm not hungry" was never an accepted response to food offering when it came to answering the aunts.

Diego did not seem to notice Charlie transporting him to the area they slept in the common room. As he laid his snoring brother down on the bed and covered him with a blanket, Charlie laughed quietly, watching some drool come out of his brother's mouth. He shook his head and thought to himself, *Diego probably looks more like mom than I do.* He kissed his brother on the head and headed out the door. As he locked up the house, Charlie took a deep breath vowing to end the night better and left the house to head back to the plaza.

As he started down the road many thoughts continued to fill his mind. His family, the aunts, the business, where his father was, and even Rene and her "war painted face." He liked her, maybe more than he had previously realized. She didn't seem to notice anything about how he was feeling that night, so that was good. As his thoughts distracted him, suddenly, a chirping call of a bat seemed to buzz right over his head. He ducked and swept the top of his curly haired head, checking to see if anything had landed in that thick nest.

What the? he thought to himself, straightening up and looking in the direction of the bat's noises. When he gazed into the distance, he saw a strange flickering light, similar to light hitting a mirror's surface. He grew suspicious and changed course of where he was headed and went towards the weak flashing light until it stopped. He continued walking along the backstreets, recalling the area where the light had come from. He soon realized he was near the cemetery where his mother was buried.

He forgot about the curious light and entered the cemetery instead.

    As he entered through the gate and closed it behind him, he noticed the bat chirping overhead again, making him look up in the direction it came from. As he scanned the branches above him, he caught a glance of the moon. It was full and bright, but some dark clouds were on their way to dim its light. Refocusing, he made his way over towards his mother's corner of the graveyard. A heavy fog was beginning to creep in between the headstones as the air grew colder. Many of the gravesites in the cemetery were decorated by loved ones for *Dia de los Muertos,* and the final few people visiting had made their way to the exit, leaving him the only one there. As he caught sight of his mother's gravesite he noticed her's was one of the few not decorated by candles and flowers. He sighed heavily, feeling sorry that her site had been neglected compared to the others. Though she was loved by her sisters deeply, running the food business to keep their heads above water didn't leave any of them much time to sit and mourn at the cemetery, especially on a particularly busy night like tonight in the village center. He carefully took a rose, a lit candle, and handful of marigold petals from a gravesite heavily decorated nearby and carried them over to his mother's place. He placed his borrowed decorations at the head of her plot that read:

Carmen Figueroa Castillo
Wife, Mother, Sister
1865-1893

"Hi, Mama," Charlie whispered at the gravesite that held his mother's remains as he sat down. "Sorry, I haven't come as much as I used to." He continued to communicate towards his mother. "Your sisters have been keeping me and Diego busy with the cooking business, I guess… We should be getting another letter from Papa soon…" He trailed off and faced the ground. Tears rolled down his nose and onto his hands as he spun his mom's gold wedding ring around on his little finger again.

"I miss you, Mama. I wish you were here and we were a family again," Charlie said softly as he wept. He sat there a while thinking of memories of them all together. Visions of her face filled his mind. He continued, "Six years is a long time, Mama, and Papa hasn't been back in five. Diego hardly knows him at all. I barely still know him…" Charlie sniffed and quickly wiped the tears off his face, angry now thinking of his father being gone. He felt the pain he lived with was equal to his father's, and it was unfair he had run off. He was stuck there, unable to escape his own memories. Charlie slammed his fist onto his knee in frustration and shook his head. He sat there in the cemetery a while in silence and closed his eyes. "I love you Mama, I'll try to visit more often," Charlie finally shared, opening his eyes as he stood up to leave, looking down where his mother lay in rest once more. The cemetery was dark now that the moon was covered by the clouds. A lot of the candles that had lit up the graves had even burned out including the one on Carmen's.

Charlie slowly made his way out of the cemetery the same way he came. As he stepped through the gate's threshold, a strong gust of wind rushed through the trees nearby, circled around the cemetery, and followed forcefully behind Charlie, pushing him forward through the threshold. The feeling as if something gave him a shove hit so suddenly caused him to quickly turn to see who or what it was. Not paying attention to his next step, he twisted his ankle stepping onto a rock falling backwards onto his behind, as his head whip lashed back and hit the ground. The fall knocked him out momentarily when a strong pressure came down on his chest, causing him to gasp for air, suddenly waking him up. He blinked rapidly and opened his eyes to see the moon back in view as the black clouds moved on.

"Isn't this a great night?" Charlie sneered sarcastically as he propped himself upon his elbows looking around at the ground, checking to see what he might have tripped over. As he scanned the grounds, something caught his eye on his right. He rolled over to get a closer look at the item peeking up out of the grass. He sat on his knees and reached out to pick it up.

ZAP The item seemed to shock him instantly.

"Ouch. What the? What is this?" Charlie questioned out loud. He reached into his back pocket for his father's handkerchief to pick up the mysterious item. As he opened his clothed hand, there was Rene's necklace, chain and all. He recalled seeing it on her at the *quinceañera* and from time to time there after. It was unique, just like Rene, he thought.

Oh no. Rene must've lost this, Charlie told himself. *She's gonna be upset, or worse, her parents.*

Charlie quickly stood up putting the wrapped necklace in his pocket and began to dust himself off when he began to feel dizzy. He stepped back and nearly lost his balance, remembering he had just been knocked out.

"Woah," He called out in his daze as the ground below him spun for a moment. He grabbed his head and rubbed the back side of it. As he ran his fingers through his hair, he felt something wet. "No way," he whined, bringing his hand forward to look at. "And now I'm bleeding!" Charlie huffed, rolling his eyes. He quickly wiped the blood off his hand on the inside of his pants pocket and stomped off towards the town square to help his aunts, who were probably wondering where he had been.

Back at the Rameriz-Lombardi house, Rene and Ana sat outside in the backyard nearby Gilberto's lit up pizza oven for warmth.

"Woman, I know I'm not your Ma. I'm your friend and I am looking out for you!" Rene shot back at Ana's 'you're not my mother' comment. "I mean, I just chased down a demon wearing my father's Samurai armor to the cemetery, but it's… whatever. Not important. I'll just run around all night helping people on my birthday I guess. That's what life is looking like for me now," Rene rambled on walking towards the darkness of the night with a shrug as her arms crossed her chest.

"Why did you put on your papa's armor? It looks old and smelly." Ana chimed in, confused as she reflected on what Rene just shared.

"No. The demon possessed it. I didn't wear it. I was still in my bloomers... My *chonies* basically!" Rene laughed, swinging her dress around to face Ana throwing her hands in the air.

"*Chonies!*" Ana hollered and erupted in laughter, exciting the dogs that ran over to her and started licking and jumping on her. "No! No. No. No! Off!" Ana complained as she pushed her dogs off of her. "Ugh. My dress. Please. I only have one good dress. I don't need to smell like dog spit right now. Ew," Ana added, adjusting her dress and dusting off the dog's hairs and dusty paw prints.

"If you were taller, you could have all mine," Rene laughed at the situation as she walked over to sit by Ana on the bench.

"Yeah. Only like six more inches to grow," Ana joked. "That's not happening. Maybe Cristiana might grow tall like Papa and you," Ana added as she looked over at Rene and gasped. "Your necklace. Ren! Where is it?"

"Oh no!" Rene whispered with concern. Rene grabbed at her bare neck and quickly stood back up. She started searching around on the floor. Ana stood and joined in the search as well. There was only so much area lit up from the oven's fire to see anything. As Rene was ready to run off in the night to look for her necklace, Ana quickly grabbed her arm holding her back.

"No, Ren, don't!" Ana advised quickly. "It's dark, and you already fought a samurai. We will look tomorrow. I promise to help you. I think we had enough today."

"Okay. Tomorrow," Rene said with a heave and nodded in agreement with Ana. She was still unsettled but did her best to let it go for now.

"We'll find it. Maybe it fell off in your fight by the cemetery," Ana brainstormed as she took the ribbon out of her hair.

A flashback crossed Rene's mind, and the sound of the demon's laugh rising out of the Samurai filled her thoughts again. A sense of fear started to creep in that she hadn't felt before.

"Maybe," Rene repeated in a somewhat trance-like state as she dazed out into the trees past Ana's house. She wondered where that spirit was now.

"Ren!" Ana shouted, clapping her hands in Rene's ear to snap her out of it. "Come on; let's go to bed. You're creeping me out a little." Ana whined with a shiver as she turned to go into the house.

"Oh. Sorry," Rene apologized, shaking her head to refocus and followed behind.

"Ren… Reeen… Reeeen," Ana nagged the next morning, shaking Rene's shoulder gently till her eyes opened. "Crazy dreams again?" Ana added, watching her friend's mysterious eye color fade from bright green to their usual hazel. She was used to her seeing her eyes change by now, as they did that more often the past year. Rene face-palmed herself, worried she'd done something odd or embarrassing in her sleep again.

"What did I do this time?" Rene sighed as she rolled over away from Ana.

"Oh. Nothing," Ana said, shrugging her shoulders. Rene looked at her confused as Ana continued, "Your eyes were changing again when you woke up. But, I mean, you said, 'Find Charlie.'

But that's it. Is he lost?" Ana asked, scrunching her eyebrows and tilting her head to the side, also looking confused now.

"I hope not," Rene replied as she stood up quickly from their sleepover area of blankets on the floor of the common room. She quickly gathered her things as Ana followed suit cleaning up the room.

"Okay…? So find your necklace, find Charlie… making a list I guess…" Ana rambled on counting her fingers out as she picked up the blankets and pillows from the floor waiting for her friend to tell her something useful.

"Ah! My necklace. I forgot!" Rene replied in a hurried voice looking at Ana. "Thank you for remembering."

Ana saluted Rene and told her they could probably find Charlie's address at her mom's office in his health file. Rene didn't like the idea of looking up his private info, but something told her to find him, and she mentioned it in her sleep. It had to be important.

The girls grabbed some *pan dulce* from the kitchen for breakfast and ran off into town towards Dr. Rameriz's office. Ana huffed along behind Rene and eventually caught up at her mother's office where Rene was waiting.

"No fair, you got those long legs, Ren," Ana wheezed, as she got up to the door and pulled on the handle, when it suddenly flung open from the other side.

"Woah! Easy!" Ana hollered angrily. Rene stopped the door with the toe of her boot before it hit Ana in the face, barely missing her small, pointy nose.

"Who in the...?" the voice grunted from the other side of the door as they shoved it to get out of the doctor's office.

Rene slowly let the door slide open and carefully moved Ana out of the way. Ana was ready to start swinging at whoever was barging through her mother's office like that when Charlie appeared.

"Charlie. Hey. What's going on?" Rene quickly asked, trying not to sound awkward since they were just about to dig up his information. Ana took a deep breath to calm herself and her asthma as she cleared her angry mind.

"Oh. Rene. Ana. Sorry about that," Charlie stammered in surprise, trying to shake off his own bad mood, when Ana finally interjected.

"I gotta check in with my ma real quick. Be right back!" Ana shared in a hurry and ran in the office. Rene watched her run into the office before looking back at Charlie.

"Hey. I was gonna come find you today. I found this," Charlie quickly told Rene, as he reached in his pocket to pull out the necklace wrapped in the handkerchief. "This is yours, right?" he added as he opened his hand exposing the winged trinket.

"Oh, Thank God! Thank you, Charlie," Rene heaved in relief, taking the necklace from the handkerchief.

"I was going to look for this with Ana right after telling her mother our plans. Phew! I don't know what my parents would have said if I came home without it," Rene told Charlie in both panic and relief.

"Yea...Sure...You got it," Charlie replied with an annoyed tone in his voice. He then rolled his head back along his shoulders as he rolled them back too. A strange smell of ash then crossed Rene's nostrils. Something inside told her it came from Charlie. She looked over at him as he looked off towards the plaza and closed his eyes in pain for a moment.

"Are you okay?" Rene questioned with concern. He had never spoken to her in this tone before, and she sensed something was wrong. Other than the fact he just came out of the Doctor's office, something seemed off about him. She did her best to be patient for a response but inquired further as he finally answered, speaking simultaneously.

"Were you here to see the doctor Charlie? Or...?" she began.

"There was a wait. So I was just leaving. I'll be fine," he replied, sounding more irritated than before as he looked down at the ground to avoid eye contact with her.

"Oh, I'm sorry. Hope you feel better," Rene said as she reached out to touch his arm, knowing this usually assured people when she did.
"*Aye!*" Charlie exclaimed, as he pulled his arm away from Rene's touch. It felt like something was burning him. He quickly gripped his arm where her hand had made contact with him. As he looked over at his arm, his eyes appeared completely black for a moment, and Rene quickly took notice. "I fell last night in the cemetery, I hurt my arm," he lied. "Sorry, Rene. I gotta go to work now." Charlie smiled awkwardly with the corner of his mouth and ran off across the courtyard. As he turned away and ran from her, she noticed some dried blood on the back of his neck. She scrunched her eyebrows in wonder of what happened to him.

"Okay. Bye. Thanks again!" Rene finally hollered out in delay.

As Charlie disappeared out of Rene's eyesight into the village's growing crowd for the day, a vision suddenly flashed through her mind: Charlie's black eyes with tears rolling down the corners, followed by wind moving through the trees of the cemetery, as the sound of the menacing laugh of the demon from last night filled her mind. She gasped in shock, stepping back from where she stood as a chill was sent down her spine. She looked back out in the direction Charlie ran and stood in silence just as Ana exited the office.

He had to have been near the cemetery last night, Rene quickly told herself as she gently shook her attention away from the vision.

"Ren? Where'd Charlie go?" Ana finally questioned, looking first at Rene then in the direction of her gaze into the plaza, her eyebrows perplexed. Rene's heart sank as her eyes slowly widened, raising her eyebrows.

"That. Wasn't. Charlie," she slowly exhaled without a blink.

Chapter 11
The Unseen

Rene calmly and quickly explained to Ana what just happened between her and Charlie. She left out the darker details so she would not completely creep out her friend.

"So what do we do now? We found Charlie and your necklace, so that's good. Was your necklace ok?" Ana questioned, looking around on Rene's neck for it.

Rene lifted her hand out to Ana and opened it. She already was focused on her next course of action, the wheels in her mind turning quickly. Ana gently picked up the necklace and looked it over. She found the part of the chain that had opened up, and with her tiny crafty fingers, linked it back together.

"There. Fixed. Good as new." Ana smiled, proud of herself for fixing the necklace with ease. Rene shook her head to break her train of thought trance she was in, turning to Ana and the necklace.

"Oh thank God, Ana," Rene sighed with relief and a smile as she turned, and Ana secured it back around Rene's neck.

"Hey, it's warm," Rene said, surprised, placing her hand over the winged charm around her neck. She turned around to face Ana, who quickly looked down in confusion at the necklace.

"Warm? It felt cold to me," Ana shrugged. "Maybe it's happy to be back with you," she added with a chuckle. Rene shrugged but thought of Reina for a moment. A gust of wind blew by the two, sending Ana's curls up in the air.

"Geez! This hair!" Ana whined, gathering her hair into her hands. "Well, I'm gonna go in and help my ma and get out of this wind, ok?"

"Oh yeah. Of course, go. Charlie said there was a wait in there and didn't see the doctor. Go," Rene encouraged Ana.

"What?" Ana asked in shock. "A wait? There's a wait because my mom DID see Charlie…"Ana was annoyed. "She had just put away his file when I got in there, and you guys were out here. Why would he lie?" Ana pondered as she scrunched her eyebrows and pursed her lips.

"Embarrassed maybe?" Rene shared.

"I'm gonna find out!" Ana said sternly as she quickly turned and reentered the office.

As soon as the office door closed, Rene bolted to her family's shop. The shop had started opening earlier over the past year once Javier and Julia allowed Tomás to start cutting hair in the back room of the shop some days. They also started offering a free cup of coffee if a customer bought a painted mug before 10am. Business was good for the Reyes Tesoros shop.

Rene quickly caught her breath and pushed her wild hairs around her face behind her ears in an attempt to tidy herself before facing her parents. With her bag of clothes in one hand, she reached out for the shop door with the other, hoping that nothing seemed out of place since the fight with the Samurai the night before. The shop bell rang as her parents both looked up at Rene at the door. They smiled at once, realizing it was her.

"Good morning, *Mija*." Javier and Julia greeted Rene one after another.

"Good morning, *Papi*. Good morning, Mama." Rene walked over to her parents in different areas of the shop to greet them each with a kiss on the cheek. When Rene passed by the Samurai armor, she gave it a quick sideways glance and let out a small sigh.

"Long night, *Mija*?" Javier chimed in, as Rene set her bag down behind the counter. Rene stood up quickly and faced her father. She quickly looked over at her mother, who was still focused on arranging things in the shop, and back at her father. Javier looked over at Julia too, who had her back towards the two, and then back at Rene.

"Tomás is here. Let's say hi," Javier suggested nodding his head towards the back of the shop. They walked down the hall, passing the storage room on the right where Rene hid ready to attack the night before. She spotted the sword she had used up on the shelf where she had returned it as the events of last night quickly flashed through her mind. They quickly reached the door on the left of the hall. This one had a glass window on it, unlike the solid panel doors for the other storage rooms. This was Tomás' new workroom.

"We put this up early this morning," Javier shared as he opened the door where Tomás was inside.

As the door handle turned and Javier stepped in Tomás' "shop," Tomás turned around from arranging his countertop of barber tools.

"Hey, Rene!" Tomas said excitedly. "Good morning! What do you think of my new door?"

"It's great, *Tio*. Now we can see you back here," Rene answered with a smile as she walked over to her uncle for a hug. The room was small but big enough for Tomás to perform his barber duties. Barbering seemed to suit Tomás well, he had been happier these days and drinking less.

"Thanks. Yeah. It's coming along back here," Tomás beamed with a nod. "Thanks again, *Hermano*. Now I just need a window outside and a bench for waiting customers." Tomas winked at his brother. Javier sighed with a smirk and nodded, and he motioned at Rene to come with him.

"See you later, *Tio*," Rene stated as she turned to follow Javier back out into the hall, gently closing the door behind her.

"I might have to replace this door next," Javier added as he placed his hands in his pockets, looking at Rene as she turned to face him. He motioned towards the shop's back door with his head.

Rene lifted her eyebrows, noticing the dent in the door she hadn't paid attention to last night. She saw the Samurai shoulder check the door but hadn't realized there was any damage done. Rene looked at Javier in silence a moment, when the front door bell rang and Julia greeted whoever was there. Javier opened the back door, motioning for Rene to exit as he followed her out. As Javier closed the door to the back alley way

157

of the shop, Rene spotted two of the family horses tied at the post. Javier still took them out for a ride in the mornings and must have not taken them home afterward. The two horses whinnied in excitement at the sight of Rene, as she walked over to say hi to them.

"Well? What happened? I have a feeling you know, Rene," Javier finally inquired calmly but sternly.

Rene slowly stopped petting one of the horse's faces, as she held it next to hers and went over to face her father. In what seemed to be 'in all one breath,' she told him everything that had happened the night before. Javier listened intently, nodding, acknowledging, sighing, and scratching his head as Rene spoke. She didn't leave anything out.

"Aye, *Mija*. That was a long night," Javier replied when she finished. "Well, now I know about the door. Your mom thinks Tomás and I hit it when putting up HIS door this morning." Javier chuckled, motioning back over at the door. "We'll leave it at that. I don't want her throwing that armor out. She never liked it here to begin with, I'm sorry it gave you trouble," Javier apologized, walking over beside Rene, and put his hand on her shoulder as she went back to petting the horse beside her. Rene humbly nodded, acknowledging her father, but stayed silent. She was exhausted with everything on her mind.

"You've seemed to become a better warrior than I have ever been, Rene. Your fighting skills are beyond anything I have taught you," Javier continued.

"They weren't enough though, *Papi*. I fear the evil spirit is now in Charlie and I don't know how to fight that way," Rene immediately shared back with concern..

"*Sí, Mija.* That's a spiritual battle, not just physical," Javier suggested, but Rene sensed a lack of confidence.

"Maybe Esther?" Rene proposed, looking her father in the eye.

"Sí, go see Esther. Take the horses home for me and pay her a visit. I will stay here with your mother to help," Javier instructed with a sense of urgency.

Rene nodded, kissed her dad on the cheek goodbye, as he placed his hat on her head and told her to take that home too. Rene mounted the beautiful white horse, named Blanco, nearest to her, as her father handed her the reins of the spotted brown and cream colored horse named Splash. Rene nodded at her father and set off in a low trot back to the *posada*. As she crossed through the plaza, she heard Ana's voice calling out to her. Rene looked around for her friend when Ana suddenly popped up on the ledge of the plaza's large fountain.

"Ren! Here!" Ana hollered, waving her arms in the air as Rene spotted her and turned in her direction with the two horses, carefully navigating through the growing swarms of pedestrians and merchants.

"Mama's mad. I was snooping through Charlie's file. I was coming to tell you what I found!" Ana quickly told Rene as she approached her. Her face looked red and flustered.

"*Papi* has me taking the horses home; let's go," Rene instructed, pulling Splash around beside Ana, and motioned to her to get on.

Ana belly flopped on top of the horse and eventually got up in the saddle as Rene did her best not to laugh. "She's a little bigger than the donkey at home," Ana chuckled, as she straightened herself out and pulled up a straw hat onto her head. "I grabbed this thing on my way out of the office because of the wind!" Ana shared, tightening the strings around her neck.

Once the two girls carefully cut through the bustling village, they took off in full gallop on the horses back to Rene's house. Rene rode confidently but looked back periodically at Ana who rode a little more 'animated' to put it nicely. There was a series of whoops, hollers, and one person conversations Ana had herself, and Splash, but she did well keeping up with Rene.

After putting the horses away in the barn behind the *posada*, Ana was finally able to share with Rene what went down at her mother's office as they began to walk back towards the town to visit Esther.
"He broke a table in the exam room, Rene. My mom said he was really angry that he got hurt last night," Ana began to share.

"He hurt his arm, he said." Rene added with uncertainty, looking over at Ana as they continued down the road. "He flinched when I reached out and touched it, but it seemed more like I burned him maybe."

"Nothing about his arm was in there. Just his head. My mom wrote he seemed feverish and was sweating when he arrived," Ana added. "She went on to examine the back of his head, and that's when he growled and put his fist into the table by the exam bed," Ana said with a shiver. "She saw a contusion and a small cut that seemed to scab up already on the back of his head."

"I saw that too." Rene quickly shared. "Well, a little stream of dried blood on the back of his head when he walked away."

"Maybe he hurt his arm breaking the table?" Ana questioned, putting her fingers to her chin and squeezed her lips like a fish as she drifted in thought. She quickly became distracted by some people crossing their path ahead.

Why did he growl? Rene thought to herself. *Strange.* Rene noticed Ana had become sidetracked by the people ahead she'd been gazing at.

"Hey. Thanks, Ana. Sorry Mama got mad at you though. Doctor/patient secrets. You know that," Rene sighed, smiling at her friend.

"Right. I know," Ana said, somewhat disappointed in herself looking down. "Luckily she didn't get hurt though!" Ana added with concern, quickly looking over at Rene with her eyes wide.

"True. Charlie doesn't seem like the violent type at all. He's big but… seems like he wouldn't hurt a fly," Rene added with a shrug.

As the two got closer to the village, Rene told Ana she had to go see Esther as she and her father previously agreed upon. Ana wanted to come along with Rene for the visit, but Rene advised against it, suggesting Ana just go ahead and spend time with her other friends that had caught her eye moments ago. Ana sighed, half relieved, sharing that she'd probably have enough excitement already for the day. She scurried off towards the familiar faces in the distance.

When Rene arrived at the church, she found Esther in her office sitting at her desk looking at a piece of paper that looked like a letter. Colors from the stained glass reflected across the desktop, and a worn looking envelope was nearby looking as if it had come a long way to be there.

"Rene. Good morning. What can I do for you today?" Esther quickly asked, as she folded the letter and put it back in the envelope, sensing some urgency from her young friend at her door.

"Good morning, Esther. I'm sorry to interrupt. Do you need a minute?" Rene quickly replied.

"No, I was done. My sister in Italy… haven't heard from her in a while, but everything is fine." Esther smiled gently, tapping the letter on the desk. "What about you? No books today?" Esther noted curiously, motioning at Rene's empty hands as she stood and walked towards Rene.

"Oh Um. No, Sister. This visit wasn't planned," Rene stammered as a vision of her bag she left at the shop this morning with her books inside crossed her mind.

"I see," Esther added, sensing more concern in Rene's voice. "Come in, sit down. Tell me what's happened, and happy belated birthday," Esther told Rene as she closed the door behind them.

For the third time since the possessed Samurai attacked and seemed to dissipate into the air, Rene told the story to her *comadre*. She included every detail and left no questions Esther had unanswered. The ones she could answer anyway. She told her about the boy named Charlie and what he had gone through, as far as she and Ana had puzzled together with the doctor's notes and Rene's encounter with him that morning.

"Your father may be right, *Mija*. This is going to be a spiritual battle for your friend," Esther concluded.

"That's why I'm here. You said in time you'd help me heal a mind. I need to learn sooner now. First Ana, now Charlie," Rene reminded Esther urgently.

"Yes, Rene. We have two different cases at hand. Ana suffers from a traumatic childhood experience but is also seeking love and approval in similar ways that are unhealthy and won't be fulfilling long term. By not being selective in her relationships, she chooses to surround herself sometimes with people who will give her attention, good or bad. Unfortunately, time and learning healthy habits will be what heals her mind. The unfavorable memories of her abuse that pains her will fade out in time. The pain anyway. The memory of it entirely, no." Esther explained.

"Yes, Sister, I remember you saying that," Rene replied. "Like an injury that heals and pain still comes out of it even after it's scarred over. In time, the pain stops, but the scar still remains."

"Correct. But for Charlie. If he is possessed as you suspect, we will see in time. The less time that spirit stays in him, the better off he will be," Esther shared in a tone of warning, rising from her desk. "His future is more uncertain, Rene. Come, let's find a book downstairs."

They exited the office and hurried their way down the hall and stairwell to the room where Rene would study books of the past. As the door creaked open, the candles and torches in the room lit up by Rene's presence as they did everytime she entered that "dungeon." The two hurried down the wooden stairs leading into the room, the room echoing back the sounds of their footsteps across the stone floor. Since Rene had spent more time there studying, Javier built a bigger desk and more shelves for books in the room for her. This way, books could stay out and not have to go back underground every study session. Even some of the Reyes' books from home even made their way into the room too.

"I've read all these books, Sister. What are we looking for?" Rene questioned Esther, as she stopped following her across the room.
"Yes, every book you know of you've read, but these you haven't," Ether shared, lowering her voice as she crossed the room to the far wall.
She picked up a torch out of a sconce with one hand, looked back at Rene, and back at the wall. With Esther's free hand, she covered it with the sleeve of her habit and reached up to touch the sconce, pressing it forcefully into the wall. There was a loud click, followed by a release where a stone wall panel popped forward out of place. Rene's jaw dropped as Esther pulled the

door open along the protruding seam. A large cobweb covered the doorway, causing Esther to look back at Rene.

"No spiders for me, Rene. Please," Esther said as she motioned for Rene to go in first to get rid of the web.

Rene picked up a small hand broom at the desk she'd kept there for dusting off books when she came to study. As she gently collected the webs onto the broom bristles, a bookshelf no more than an arms length from the door's entry was revealed.

"These books may never leave this room, Rene, for any reason, at all," Esther warned as Rene began looking over the book spines. She noticed they had symbols on them, unlike the books from the underground shelf. Rene eventually nodded in agreement.

"Let me see. Take this," Esther instructed Rene, handing her the torch. Esther pulled up her robes as she kneeled down on the ground to take a book from the bottom shelf.
"Here it is," Esther stated, holding an old black book with a black string embroidery around the edge. Esther took her sleeve again, covered her hand, and wiped the cover clean.

The Unseen, the title read.

Esther turned at the waist and held the book up for Rene to take.

"These books are dark, Rene. Not like the darkness of unfortunate events you've read about before," Esther shared as she got up from the floor, looking at the book in Rene's hand, taking the torch back. "I didn't want a young girl like you to be getting into these, but if you've learned about the light, you're going to need to know about the dark too, I fear." Esther finished with a heavy sigh as she shook her head gently.

Rene nodded, as she cracked open the book and started thumbing through the pages and walked over to the desk and chair. As Esther closed the wall door, the sconce popped back out into its position where she returned the torch into its place.

Rene learned about demonic spirit possession from *The Unseen*. She was mindful to remember to return it and any other book she'd taken out of the wall library to read, heeding Esther's warning. She did well to not tell Ana or her Father about this new library Esther shared with her, out of concern that they may not be able to handle it or would worry about her.

She learned that these unseen spirits can be triggered to appear when a nearby human had little faith and enough negative emotions for them to cling to; like sadness, desperation, and anger, for example. These were favored conditions they fed on. These spirits, while on a day where loved ones were being remembered like *Dia de los Muertos* were known to find their own opportunities to be "born again." These forgotten souls linger, hoping to be "invited" to the human realm again, releasing them from the dark realm they wait in. These spirits, though not invited willingly or knowingly by humans, could break through to Rene's realm. When they sense a strong light presence, they'll have trouble clinging to a human host. This was the case for Ana, twice while Rene was near, on her past two birthdays. Since Rene was not present in Charlie's case, the evil spirit had, indeed, latched on to his soul to overtake. Black eyes, increased strength, anger, and the scent of ash and fire were there as signs of possession in *The Unseen*, confirming Rene's suspicion.

Rene grew concerned for Charlie at the thought of his becoming ultimately soulless as the spirit dwelled in him. She had to find out how she would be able to expel the spirit from Charlie and soon. This would also require Charlie to even acknowledge that he was even possessed in the first place. As the demon works tirelessly to prove they are not two but only one spirit dwelling in the soul, this would make things more difficult.

As Rene became wiser with her studies over the next couple months, Charlie also became more in harmony with the spirit dwelling in him. This was convenient for the host but not the people around him. His aunts grew tired of his disrespect towards them and his lack of care towards his little brother, which was so out of character for him. He grew cold and distant from his family and friends. He made new friends that seemed just as corrupt as he was becoming. Some were known troublemakers and even considered "lost souls" in the village, as the residents would describe them. He was getting into fights with other teenagers, and sometimes grown men would end up at Dr. Rameriz's office with a wound or broken bone. Rene kept her distance from Charlie but also tried to find any opportunity to get near to rouse the demon spirit inside to break their harmony, alerting Charlie of its presence. This new study had Rene's usual confidence level at an unusual "low" which inconveniently delayed the assistance she could offer Charlie. She did her best to take thought out actions that would help him.

  Coincidentally or perhaps divinely ordained, Diego and Cristiano soon became friends. They were similar in age, and Diego loved playing with the inventions Cristiano created, which is how they met. Cristiano had made a toy that accidentally took off and rolled under the *Figueroa Cocineras* food stand one day where Diego was sitting, playing with some toy figures his aunts had made him. Rene saw it as an opportunity to get insight on

Charlie and encouraged the friendship. Rene would walk Cristiano to Diego's house every so often or even just took them both out for the day to play by the river or somewhere outdoors. Diego thanked Rene for being like a big sister to him since Charlie didn't seem to care for him anymore.

"He's a 'Teenager,' the aunts say," Diego shared, walking home with Cristiano one day. Rene followed the two closely enough to hear the conversation.

"What happens to teenagers?" Cristiano asked with concern "Ren is a teenager!" He added, looking back at his sister with wide eyes before looking back at Diego. He had picked up on Ana's nickname for his sister and decided to call her that too.

"He comes home late. Forgets where he was. Yells at the Aunts," Diego rambled on, throwing his hands up in despair with a sigh, looking like his aunts, no doubt.

"Oh. That's scary. We can't yell at grown ups. Unless they are bad and hurting us," Cristiano replied, shaking his finger like Julia would do when she was teaching him a lesson.
"Charlie is scary. I'm scared to be a teenager. I don't want to be a mean bully like that!" Diego exclaimed. "They said they might send him to Papa if he doesn't get better. I heard them. They thought I was asleep." He finished in a whisper.

"Where's your Papa at?" Cristiano questioned innocently, as Rene tuned in more for the answer as well.

"'Merica, somewhere. Working," Diego shrugged as he kicked a rock lying on the ground.
"He helps farmers or something. Keeps his mind off Mama. That's all the aunts say. He didn't have family around here

except me and Charlie. Those are Mama's sisters." Diego rambled on openly.

"What happened to your Mama, Diego?" Cristiano went on to ask when Rene chimed in suddenly.

"Ok, 20 questions are up, Cris," Rene warned, worried Diego would get upset by the question.

"She got killed. I don't remember her that much, I was a baby. But… Charlie and the Aunts?" Diego sighed. "Don't even talk about her!" He finished, shaking his head. Cristiano nodded looking concerned and saluted Diego. Rene laughed inside remembering the time she saluted Charlie as the vision sparked through her mind.

"OK soldiers, let's go home now," Rene announced, picking up the pace ahead of them with her long legs. The two little boys scurried along quickly behind her like ducklings following their mother.

Chapter 12
The Kingdom

Spring 1900

In the weeks that followed, things in Puebla grew chaotic to say the least. For Rene, her dreams grew untamed once again like they did in past years. They had become manageable so long as she prayed beforehand, but even with her book of prayers she kept growing beside her bed, these dreams were unruly.

She dreamt of Charlie's family before his mother's murder tore them apart. He had been there when the men attacked his parents coming home from work one night. His Dad told him to run for help as he held his bleeding wife in his arms. It was a stab wound to her stomach causing her to bleed to death. Others came to aid the Castillo's in their quarrel with the men and capturing the attackers who ultimately died in prison from their wounds. Unfortunately, there was no saving Carmen or young Charlie's heart from breaking.

Some days, Rene would wake up in tears and deep feelings of sorrow for what Charlie's family had gone through. It also gave her a deeper appreciation for her own family and joy that each day was another chance to make memories with them.

However, Rene's 'new' books to study came with their own set of nightmares to torment her at night. She'd waken from only a startling dream or two before she stopped having Ana sleep over or sleeping over at Ana's. Worried for her young student, Esther suggested taking a break from the Dark Books, she called them, but Rene refused. She was resolute in her decision to learn about the mind and the effect people and evil spirits had on it. Esther reminded her to keep her studies of *the light* just as close. She devoted time to study each equally to keep her own mind balanced. This advice Rene found most beneficial and did eventually level out her dreams by spring.

Spring was Ana's favorite season, even though the pollen in the air didn't help with her asthma. Rene and Ana spent time together during the days more since nights were off limits for now. Though Ana wasn't as athletically inclined as Rene, they both still enjoyed the outdoors. Rene took the time to share some of her studies about the light to help Ana heal her mind. Rene would let Ana read her prayer book from time to time, hoping they would help clear the cobwebs of her mind that filled her with doubts and insecurities causing her to make impulsive decisions. Of course, at times where Rene was off climbing a nearby tree or swimming in the river, Ana would become distracted and would draw in Rene's book of prayers. She'd often draw a small bird that Rene would always point out especially in spring resembling Reina. Ana knew Rene wouldn't mind seeing that little bird drawing scattered across the pages of her book, and she was right. Ana would argue that books are better with pictures anyways, since, of course, Ana loved art. She was really good too. Even the little bird sketches in Rene's book that Ana effortlessly drew looked realistic. Ana called Reina "Rene's happy thought" and felt the prayer book was a great place to be remembered.

Ana eventually began attending church with Rene too, sometimes for service and sometimes for prayer and candle lighting. Ana felt uplifted and inspired a lot afterwards too, maybe not every time but a good portion of the time. Church also would upset her, seeing where she was struggling and where she still needed to do work. She didn't like that part of The Word. Like many others, there were parts that were easy to accept and left the rest rejected, for a while anyway.

"God isn't here to clean up after us. He warns us to not make a mess by being hasty in our actions," Rene would remind Ana. Loving her all the same, clean or messy, was what He would always do, Ana ultimately learned. That comforted her. Rene was happy to see her friend's life and happiness improve, but there was still Charlie out there, spiraling out of control.

The *Figueroa Cocineras* business began struggling over the past few months with Charlie's new disruptive and hostile behavior. He was easily angered and snapped at anyone who gave him any direction or slightest complaint about the food, no matter how nicely they'd put it. His aunts feared for their nephew, wondering what would become of him in the future if he didn't change soon. Rene would get updates at times from Cristiano and Diego's conversations as Charlie seemed to avoid Rene more.

"I saw Charlie taking money from *Tia* Olivia's room the other day. He doesn't know I saw," Diego shared on his walk home with Cristiano and Rene one day in a low disappointed tone. "The aunts know he's up to something though. They're gonna catch him soon," Diego warned, shaking his finger and scrunching his eyebrows. Cristiano nodded his head in agreement.

"Stealing is bad, huh Ren?" he asked his sister, looking back at her on their walk home from the river.

"Right, Cris. We need to make our own money from working if we want it," Rene replied sternly.

"Mama and Papa are going to let me help at the shop when I'm ten," Cristiano shared proudly with his friend.

"Charlie is supposed to work to help the aunts; he told me before. I guess I'll do that too one day. But I don't want to cook. The kitchen is too hot," Diego whined in response briefly when something in the cemetery caught his eye. He squinted as he gazed ahead. Rene looked up to see what Diego was trying to focus on.

Charlie. Rene told herself. *There he is.* Rene quickly thought to distract the boys.

"Hey did you see that? That hawk was huge!" Rene lied pointing skyward, causing the boys to look up.

"Where!?" The boys said in unison with excitement.

"It flew ahead, looked like it was headed for the barn. I hope the chickens are locked up!" Rene continued to fib. "Cris, go check. Hurry. I'll catch up with you," Rene instructed. Cristiano nodded and motioned to Diego to follow him home in full sprint. She watched the two run off in the distance before making her way over to Charlie at the cemetery.

Rene treaded lightly as she got closer to Charlie at the cemetery. With her eyes focused and ears tuned in on him, trying to pick up on what was going on before she got closer. There was a heavy wind blowing in the tree's canopy that was rustling the leaves and limbs that hindered Rene's ability to clearly hear Charlie's conversation at the grave site. It was between two people but in only Charlie's voice.

Is he talking to himself? Out loud? Rene asked herself. She hid behind a tree and closed her eyes hoping to give more focus power to her hearing.

"Sacrifices have to be made," an evil hiss-like voice demanded.

"There is no other way?" Charlie's tired voice questioned.

"This is the fastest way to get it done," the dark voice harshly spoke again.

"I'm tired. I need sleep." Charlie muttered to himself.

He's arguing with it. That's a good sign. Rene thought.

"Hey, Charlie!" Rene quickly announced, as she whipped around the tree, giving Charlie a startle as he looked up at her. "I thought that was you over here," Rene said with a smile, trying to not let on that she had been overhearing his conversation.

As Rene focused on Charlie, she saw his eyes change. His iris was black and abnormally large, just as she had pictured them before. This was also a sign of possession that she'd read about. Charlie quickly blinked, causing his eyes to cool and return to their hazel, earthly tones resembling Rene's.

"Rene, hey, what are you doing here?" Charlie quickly asked, looking around the cemetery. It was as if he'd forgotten where he was. Rene approached him confidently and fearlessly as she felt her necklace begin to warm up against her skin.

Standing strong in your faith with fearlessness protects you. She recalled reading in her books about dealing with dark spirits.

"I was walking the boys home and thought I saw you here. Thought I'd say hi," She said as friendly as possible.

"Oh. Okay, yes you saw me," Charlie said, awkwardly looking away from Rene. "Do you have family here?" Charlie questioned her awkwardly as he began to sweat.

"Fortunately, I do not. My Tata was going to be laid to rest here, but Nana insisted on cremation like her ancestors," Rene shared as she looked around the graveyard for any signs of danger. "Who are you visiting?" Rene asked as genuinely as possible, already knowing the answer.

"Oh, I, Um." Charlie mumbled before clearing his throat, "my mother is here." Charlie admitted nodding toward his mother's plot.

"I see. I'm sorry about your loss Charlie. Must be hard?" Rene replied and did her best to be empathetic.

"I get by," Charlie quickly replied nonchalantly. He did his best to be unemotional in his answer, or was that the demon talking? Charlie started to grow uncomfortable. He started acting restless, rubbing his face and pulling at his hair as he ran his fingers through it. Rene just watched him quietly and patiently, waiting for him to speak again.

"So, why did you come by again?" Charlie questioned Rene forgetting what she had already told him. He wiped his brow that had started sweating more as Rene squatted down near a tombstone. She dusted off some leaves that fell on it trying to tone down her intimidating presence that made Charlie seem more uneasy than usual around her.

"Visiting a friend, Charlie." Rene stated as she looked at the tombstone.

"Are we friends, Rene?" Charlie asked in a relaxed tone finally.

A breakthrough, Rene thought, she enthusiastically rose up and looked Charlie in the eyes.

"I thought you might want to be?" Rene suggested with a smile and shrug. Her face appeared relaxed, but inside she was experiencing a swell of emotions.

Be calm, but be ready. She told herself. Charlie laughed.

"Friends. Yeah. That's what I need," He said sarcastically with a scoff.

Lost him again. Rene thought, closing her eyes in disappointment. *Damn.*

"The princess of Puebla and the town Pauper, 'friends,'" Charlie laughed menacingly as he began circling around Rene. Rene watched him as he circled her. He rolled his head back along his shoulders then stopped as he looked up at the sunset sky in a daze.

"Charlie, what's going on? Why are you saying things like that?" Rene questioned him calmly, knowing that there was a battle going on inside him too. She stayed as patient as possible. "Rene, I think you should go home now," Charlie said, now looking down at the ground.

"Will you come get Diego when you're done here please?" Rene asked kindly. Charlie nodded yes as he walked back to his mother's plot and sat beside it.

Charlie never came for Diego. It was after nightfall that Aunt Olivia came for Diego with her sister Maya. They had both lost their husbands as young wives at the end of the Texas-Indian wars and never remarried. They relied on each other and vowed to take care of each other ever since. Diego was disappointed he had to go home when finally they showed up . He and Cristiano were working on some toys in his room and didn't even notice how late and dark it had gotten.

Javier did not like the idea of their walking home in the dark, so he took them all home in the family wagon. The Figueroa family lived out on the edge of the city where there weren't many street lamps, and Javier felt responsible for their safety since Diego was a guest at his home. Nana Maria started chatting up a storm with Olivia, going on about cooking and recipes since their arrival, holding up their departure for a little while. Rene thanked her father for taking care of the situation, apologizing for Charlie's absence again and again as they readied the wagon and loaded up Diego and the Aunts.

"Let's hope that Charlie is safe, *Mija*," Javier reminded Rene. "The horses will get us there and back quickly," he assured his daughter.

Rene impatiently waited in her father's chair in the lobby waiting for him to return, just as he would do for her to come home at night.

Wheat is taking so long? Rene thought to herself, when suddenly the sound of horse hooves grew outside.

Rene jumped up from the chair and hurried to the door as the wagon rushed by on its way to the barn. She quickly closed the door and ran after the wagon to hear what, if anything, had happened. Something inside told her something did as she ran to her father's side as he dismounted the front seat.

"How did it go? Everything okay?" Rene asked concernedly. Javier shook his head no and sighed as he loosened the horse reins from the wagon.

"Charlie was there at the house. We found him blacked out on the floor, and he had a deep cut on his hand. No one knows how he got home or what happened to him," Javier shared in a serious tone, looking Rene in the eyes. "They suspected he was drunk, but we know that's probably not the case," he said, raising his tired eyebrows. Rene took a deep breath and nodded in agreement as she waited in silence for her father to go on.

"There is a darkness here, Rene," Javier continued as he undressed the horses, handing the reins to Rene to lead them into their stalls. "Charlie is going to be sent to his father for the summer to hopefully get straightened out," Javier shared authoritatively.

"Where's that?" Rene asked concernedly. She was worried about the spirit inside him leaving town.

"Alta, California area is all I know." Javier stated. Rene nodded in acknowledgement, remembering that's what Diego had shared about his father's whereabouts too.

"His aunt will be taking him out there and continuing on to visit her other sisters up in San Francisco afterwards. We should pray for their journey," Javier concluded, as he opened the side door of the barn ahead of Rene, motioning for her to exit ahead of him.

"We need to pray for more than that, Papi," Rene added with a sigh as she exited the barn.

"Si, *Mija*. We probably do," Javier agreed as he closed the barn door and latched the lock.

The next day, Rene visited Ana at the Doctors office, hoping that Charlie had been there at some point. Ana was sitting at the check in desk of her mother's two-room clinic. The wall behind her had shelves of patient files, and, of course, Ana had been thumbing across them in boredom when Rene walked in.

"Ren!" Ana squealed in excitement at the sight of her friend rising from her chair. Rene quickly waved in return, making her way towards Ana at the desk.

"Did you hear about…you know…" Ana whispered as Rene approached her, passing a woman looking through her bag sitting on a nearby chair.

Rene's eyes grew wide as she held her hand up in the shape of a C against her chest. Ana nodded vigorously, and Rene motioned for Ana to follow her outside.
"Charlie came by?" Rene quickly asked when Ana closed the office door behind them.

"Yeah. He was here. He got some stitches on his hand and looked really depressed," Ana shared as she put her hands on her hips and curled her lip into a frown.

"My father said he got hurt last night but didn't say how," Rene replied.

"I don't know either. He told my Ma in the exam room he didn't know how it happened either. I heard through the door," Ana shared matter-of-factly.

"He's going away now," Rene added with concern.

"Yes! He told me to tell you goodbye! How did you know?" Ana added with excitement and confusion.

"His aunt told my father last night," Rene stated, crossing her arms with a sigh, looking down at her boots.

"Well, maybe you need a break. It's not your job to watch him, Ren." Ana scolded Rene, crossing her arms, mirroring her friend.

"Yeah, probably," Rene sighed, relaxing her arms down to her sides. "I'll take a summer vacation then," Rene added sarcastically, throwing her hands in the air in frustration.

"Alright, take it easy, Ren. Don't get worked up over some guy…" Ana added with a laugh, looking at her friend. "Sound familiar?" She finished schooling her friend, smacking the side of Rene's arm. Rene looked down at her friend, side eyed, and flared her nostrils.

"Real familiar, *Amiga*," Rene snorted and pursed her lips. "Okay, well you better get back in there before your mama calls the next patient," Rene warned her friend, taking a deep breath as she thought of what to do next.

"Ok Ren, see you later," Ana chuckled and rolled her eyes playfully.

Rene spent the early summer working harder than ever, both mentally and physically. There were no vacations for the evil, and she certainly wasn't taking one either. She did her best to balance her life between working at the shop, playing with her brother, friend, and praying at the church with Esther. However, it turned out that her parents had plans of their own for Rene. They planned to take Rene to Italy on their next trip with Cristiano. Though his eye troubles had been cleared, he would still need a new glass eye fitted for his naturally growing socket over the years.

Julia had caught a glimpse into Rene's prayer book when she left it at the shop back in November. It had fallen out of her bag when she went to move it out of the way behind the counter. Though she appreciated the thoughtfulness of her daughter's words, she also was concerned that with all the time Rene spent caring and thinking of others, she would forget to prioritize herself. As was true in Julia's own life as a wife, mother, and business owner. Her daughter grew up fast as a child through whatever divine forces brought her to be here, but she didn't need to rush growing up her whole teenage life either.

As the month of June quickly came and went, Rene knew it was coming up for her parents and brother to travel to Italy again. Maybe she was so busy with everything on her mind, but she didn't know she'd be going along this time till Nina showed up one day at the *posada*.

"Nina?!" Rene exclaimed in surprise. "What are you doing here? Hi Alana! Wow. What a surprise." Rene was happy to have her family back again to visit.

"Mama's name is Ernestina, not Nina," Alana corrected Rene sternly. Rene laughed.

"Right. That is her name, but I call her Nina," She added with a smile looking down at Alana.

"Alana, no one calls me that. My middle name is best," Ernestina laughed, hugging Rene again.

"Rebekita! You made it!" Julia announced as she came down the hall to greet her sister. Alana shook her head at the floor, hearing yet another nickname for her mother. Julia hugged Alana's head, pressing it against her hip as she hugged her little sister at the same time.

"I can't breathe," Alana whined, pushing herself away from her aunt's leg.

"Okay, someone needs a nap!" Nina announced just as Julia stepped back from her moody niece.

"We have this room for you here," Julia motioned with a smile. "Come, let's get you settled in… Rene, get the bags please!" Julia instructed impatiently but as kindly as possible, alerting Rene.

"I didn't know they were coming to visit?" Rene questioned her mother as she gathered up Nina's bags and followed her to the room.

"It's a surprise, *Mija*," Julia added as they walked down the hall to Nina's room.

"I guess so," Rene shrugged, following behind her family.

What surprise though? Rene asked herself. As they entered the guest room and Rene set down their bags, Nina spilled the beans.

"So! Italy, Rene? Are you excited?" Nina exclaimed.

"What?" Rene asked in confusion, looking first at her aunt and then over to her mother.

"Oh, yes, we had not told Rene yet, Rebekita," Julia chuckled nervously.

"Oops!" Nina sighed with a grimace on her face.

"It's okay, *Hermana*," Julia comforted her sister with a smile before looking over at Rene. "Rene, yes, you are coming along this time to Italy," Julia shared excitedly.

"WHAT!? I AM!?" Rene shouted out in a high pitched voice. Alana quickly turned around to find out what was happening now. She had tuned out the conversation as she searched through the bags for her dolls just as Rene lunged at her mother to hug her in excitement.

"I can't believe it! Wow!" Rene shared in excitement.
"*Nina* is here to help Nana and Tomás while we're gone," Julia grunted as Rene continued to squeeze the breath out of her.

"Oh, sorry, Mama," Rene apologized with a laugh, releasing her mother from her stronghold. Alana laughed, too, as she watched the excitement come out of her big cousin.

"We've been making arrangements for you to go study out there with *Señor* Lombardi's help next year, so we thought a visit was necessary beforehand," Julia explained to Rene as she nodded affirmatively in excitement. Her eyes welled up with happy tears.

I'm going! Rene exclaimed internally as she smiled at her mother.

Ana had known about these plans, as she, of course, eavesdropped on her parents' conversations living in their small house. She couldn't help that they had thin walls and her father's large presence came with a loud voice, almost incapable of whispering. She had kept the information to herself under the warnings of her older sister, who also overheard the plans one night. This didn't make it easier on Ana when it came time to say goodbye to her friend for the summer. "Looks like you're getting a vacation after all," is what Ana told Rene as happily as possible when she shared the news.

Gilberto and Ana took the Reyes family to the Port at Veracruz to make way for "The Kingdom," as Mr. Lombardi still called it. Javier and Gilberto had become friends over the years that Ana and Rene spent 'joined at the hip,' as they would say. Javier gave permission to the Rameriz-Lombardi family to use the family wagon and his fathers small home there in Veracruz over the summer while they were gone. Ana was most excited about that part of the arrangement at least, as was Gilberto, hoping to find a more accepting job site temporarily working at the docks.

The summer flew by for the two families. Rene enjoyed her time in Italy and even met Sister Alma Maria while she was there. Turns out that even Esther, too, had a part in the Italy arrangement for her. Rene loved the history she learned in "The Kingdom" and the pizza of course, slightly different from Mr. Lombardi's style but still delicious. She was able to tour the University of Padua, where Gilberto's father, Gianluca, was a professor and was able to get Rene's entry approved for study in the spring of 1901.

Grandpa Lombardi and most of his colleagues were impressed by Rene and the education she had received by her parents and independent study she'd undertaken herself. She passed their entry examinations with ease and remained completely humble at the same time. Italy was just the vacation that Rene's mind needed, but her soul was still restless. Sister Alma was Esther's twin, as it turned out, and Rene felt equally connected to Alma as she had with Esther. Esther had shared a lot about Rene with her sister confidentially. The things she didn't, she'd quickly learn about as Rene opened up to her in their short time together. Rene would be staying in a local convent while she attended the university, so she would remain balanced in her routines even when she was far from home.

The Reyes family returned early September as promised. Alana was adamant about having everyone home for her birthday, and a small party was held for both her and Cristiano. Since they had a birthday only one day apart, it was the convenient thing to do. They were now both seven.

"Seven at last," Alana declared, as she blew out her candles with Cristiano. "Halfway to womanhood," She added with a royal attitude, causing the family to roar with laughter around the kitchen table. Rene nudged Alana with a poke to her side to snap her out of her sassiness and began to tickle her when she heard a knock at the door. It was faint behind all the excitement at the table, but, of course, she was the only one that heard it.

Who? Rene questioned as she headed for the door. As she reached for the door, the hairs on her arm stood on end. She pressed down on the thumb latch and opened the door, looking back towards her family to see if anyone had followed her.

"Hello, Rene," the voice on the other side said before she turned to see who it was.

Rene gasped, and her heart stopped.

Charlie. Rene's mind announced upon seeing his face.

CHAPTER 13
Divided Soul

"Hi, Charlie, long time no see," Rene said as politely as possible, quickly stepping outside. "They just cut the cake. Diego isn't ready to go yet. I didn't know you—" She continued as she closed the door behind her just as Charlie cut her off.

"You didn't know I was coming," Charlie said, cutting her off. "I know. I didn't know I'd get home as quickly as I did, so I offered to come for him," he shared, taking a step back, looking off into the distance before looking back at her. Rene's whole being was at work studying Charlie's presence, she quickly thought of her next step. She felt uncertain of Charlie's mental state and was sure she didn't want him in the house unless he seemed "stable."

"Well, Diego will be happy to see you, I'm sure," Rene quickly assured Charlie. "Let's go for a walk around back to the courtyard. Give him time to eat his cake; they just served it," she suggested. Motioning her hand for Charlie to follow her as she began walking around the front of the *posada*. Charlie followed closely behind.

"How was your summer with your father?" Rene began her interrogation; but was careful to sound friendly and light-hearted as possible. "Alta California, must've been different, huh?"

"Oh, yeah. it's different. It's more like a desert a lot of the time… unless you're on the farmlands," Charlie shared politely. "My father doesn't talk much, but it was nice being with him. I haven't seen him in a really long time."

Rene nodded, acknowledging Charlie as she continued to lead him around the *posada* arriving at the courtyard area. A few guests staying overnight sat in the balcony seating area just above Charlie and Rene, but didn't pay much attention to them as they entered the yard. The jacarandas that were once juvenile trees potted around the courtyard for Rene's quinceanera, were now rooted into the ground and over 20ft tall. The trees' flowers were everywhere, coloring the whole yard purple.

"Wow, this is different," Charlie announced.

"What's that?" Rene replied.

"The last time I was back here was for your party, I remember seeing you come down those stairs," Charlie motioned towards the courtyard steps as he went into a daze for a moment, thinking about that night. He quickly shook his head to snap out of the memory, hoping Rene didn't notice. "Everything was more red back here, not purple," Charlie finished speaking as he awkwardly cleared his throat, looking over at her. Rene's memory of the party flashed through her mind as well, remembering almost crashing into Charlie. She held back her chuckle.

"That's right," she said with a smile, quickly changing the subject. "Did you know the jacaranda tree came from Brazil?" Rene questioned Charlie who shook his head no. Rene continued.

"Yeah. Papa meets so many people on his travels. The man, Mr. Matsumoto, came from Japan to make friends with the different governments here. He was going to bring the cherry tree, but the altitude doesn't suit them," Rene finally finished as she looked around the courtyard calmly admiring the trees. Their floral scent filled her senses.

"The altitude seems to be making me light-headed too. Must be the long journey home or something," Charlie chuckled with a small smile as he took a deep breath in. Really, he was thinking of Rene, as he looked her over from the corner of his eyes, remembering how beautiful she was to him. Even dressed as casually as she was now, that didn't matter to him.

Light Headed? Rene told herself half suspiciously, trying to have some faith in him that maybe he really was okay, for now. She didn't suspect that he had feelings for her, even up to this moment.

"I'd like us to be friends, Rene," Charlie began. "Our brothers are, can we be too?" Charlie finished as he looked up at the trees and back over at Rene. Just then, a single purple blossom fell from the tree above and landed on Rene's shoulder.

That's different from the last time... Rene reminded herself of their last conversation in the cemetery before Charlie went away. She remained silent, hoping he would go on so she could get more insight into his overall aura. She glanced down at the blossom on her shoulder before looking over at Charlie.

"I think I was rude the last time we spoke," Charlie continued. "I'm sorry if I hurt you or something. I wasn't myself. It's kind of blurry to me," he looked down in guilt, with his hands in his pockets, as he gently brushed some fallen blossoms on the floor with his worn, dusty shoe, clearing off a patch of ground. Rene watched his foot move back and forth before answering.

"We can work on that," Rene finally answered optimistically, looking up at Charlie. Charlie looked back at her and smiled gratefully. Just then, Julia's booming laugh erupted from inside, causing Rene to quickly look up at the party going on up in the house.

"That's Mama," Rene announced with a smile. Charlie chuckled in response and looked up at the party with Rene, while still looking at her from the corner of his eyes, smiling softly.

Over the next couple of months, Rene and Charlie did become closer. Rene was careful not to open up in a way that may lead him to believe they may be more than that. When they spent time together, they were never alone. Either their brothers were there or even Ana and one other friend. Charlie did seem to get back into his old ways before he went off on his aunts and seemed demon-possessed. He went back to working with his family and seemed to work even harder than before. It had seemed as though maybe the change of scenery of Alta California, and seeing his father did some good everyone noted.

Deep down, Rene wanted to believe that Charlie was healed. Her dreams at night thought differently. Rene's dreams replayed everything that Charlie had been through that past year and the last encounter she had with him in the cemetery. She even got insight into his time with his father over the summer, part fueled by what Charlie shared with her and part imparted to her by her 'gifts,' she was looking for a particular event in her dreams of Charlie. Never finding the moment led her to believe that Charlie was a soul divided, meaning that the demon still remained in Charlie and was never released.

Rene would wake up with a thousand questions, and she would answer all that she could by re-calling her studies over the years. Even recalling the newer studies of the dark books she began this past year. However, Esther would still be the one she would confide in for a clarification or confirmation.

"I haven't seen an exit," Rene told Esther with concern. "It has to be still inside him," she speculated.

"Perhaps it's dormant," Esther stated, bringing her hand to her chin in thought leaning back in her chair looking down at her desk.

"A sleeping volcano," Rene concurred with a nod as she gazed up at the stained glass window of a dove in Esther's office.

Ana wasn't of much help with Rene's speculations, unfortunately. She accused Rene of not wanting to open up to Charlie, finding excuses to not fall in love with him. Ana found Charlie to be charming lately. He seemed helpful and sweet anytime they all hung out too. Ana, on the other hand, had fallen in love over the summer and kept in touch with her new boyfriend, Arturo, by mail. He wasn't much of a writer, he'd send a pressed wildflower with a little note to her in response to her long-winded letters, and she didn't mind. She wished Rene would spend some time swooning in love like she did instead of being so independent. Rene was, of course, happy Ana's new relationship was long distance. This way Ana was still able to focus on other things in life too, for now.

"Ana, I'm leaving in the new year, this is no time to make commitments anywhere around here. This is when I need to finish tying up loose ends," Rene reminded her friend, but also sounding like a warning.

"Loose ends, goose ends," Ana mocked back as they sat by the river side one day. "A little romance never hurt anyone," Ana continued with a smile as she wrote Arturo another letter.

"And you're proof of that!" Rene quipped, nudging her friend's pencil across her paper. Ana whipped her head to the side, giving Rene an evil look. She crumpled up her paper and proceeded to throw it at Rene's face grunting half-angrily.

"Okay, take it easy, Ana. He's going to be here before that letter gets to him in Veracruz!" Rene scoffed at her friend, throwing Ana her paper back.

"I know! I'm getting nervous. The party is next week, and I just hope he still likes me when he sees me again!" Ana squealed, stomping her feet on the ground rapidly in excitement as they sat.

"Anyway, I'll make my own decisions about Charlie. But 'friends' is the best place to start for us until I confidently know he's okay," Rene announced as she watched the river cutting over and through the rocks below them. Ana looked over at Rene then back at another piece of paper on her lap, feeling inspired.

November 1, 1900

Dia de los Muertos was upon the village in what seemed like a blink of an eye, and Rene did her best not to dread this night, as it was also her birthday.

"Seventeen!" Julia announced, abruptly entering Rene's bedroom door, striking a strange statuesque-like pose with her paints in hand, looking at the ceiling corner. Rene looked over at her mother with a cringing smile and lightly shook her head in disapproval at the same time.

"Mama, did you have coffee late again?" Rene joked, looking over at her mother who was still strangely looking off in the distance. Julia quickly snapped out of it and looked over at her daughter.

"Why yes, Rene, I sure did," she smiled, putting her hands on her hips and continued, "I think Tomás might have put something else in there though?" Julia speculated, putting her hand to her cheek. She walked over to Rene, who had just finished putting on her boots and sat down beside her. The faint scent of black licorice on her mother's breath lingered to Rene's nostrils.

Looks like I'm not the only one who's going to enjoy the festivities tonight, Rene thought with a chuckle.

"Well, really it's only been twelve years for us though," Julia quickly added as her eyes started to well up with tears. "You grew up so fast," Julia whined, grabbing a handkerchief from her apron pocket to wipe her tears before they escaped her eyes.

"Sorry, Mama," Rene answered with a smile, leaning against Julia as her mother wrapped her arms around Rene's shoulders and sighed.

"My baby," Julia added with a sniffle, holding Rene and rubbing her back a moment. Rene enjoyed the moment in silence as a gentle smile crossed her face and her body relaxed. Julia continued, "okay, let's put your makeup on!" Julia shook Rene in her arms joyfully before wiping another tear away.

"Arrgh," Rene grunted. "I thought you'd forget."

"*Amor*, you're not a pirate. That's Papa! Mama wants to do something fun for your birthday!" Julia demanded, putting her hands on her hips again as she sternly squinted her eyes at her daughter,

Rene fell back to lay on the bed and rubbed her face in desperation.

"Don't get dramatic, Rene. That's what I do!" Julia laughed half-seriously. A confused look suddenly crossed her face for a moment before shaking it off.

Probably the alcohol. Rene thought. Julia refocused and got on with her plans for Rene's look.

Julia kept her face painting more traditional and as minimal as possible for Rene. Compared to what Ana's war paint she had done the previous year, Rene sighed in relief. Julia finished her masterpiece announcing *"Fin!"* leaning back to get a final look at her daughter. Once she was satisfied with her work, she urged Rene to look over into the vanity mirror at the table.

"Oh thank God," Rene sighed with relief. "Good job, Mama. I like it." Rene looked at her face side to side in the mirror noting the small but intricate designs her mom painted around her cheeks, chin, and forehead. She then puckered her red lips out at her reflection as her eyes grew wide in shock. Julia bowed her head in gratitude with a smile and began to clean up her supplies, not noticing Rene's reactions in the mirror.

Just then Uncle Tomás barged through the bedroom door, laughing as he stumbled in.

"Julia! There you are!" Tomás declared as if he were playing hide and seek pointing at Julia. His eyes rolled around in his head like marbles in a jar.

Drunken Uncle, Rene chortled to herself.

"I told you I had to go see Rene, *Hermano!*" Julia scolded Tomás. She looked over at Rene and shook her head, standing up from the bench where the two had been sitting.

"Right. The last birthday," Tomás slurred as he crossed his arms, swaying by the door hoping to not let on how drunk he had gotten. "You're leaving us, Rene…" Tomás continued as seriously as possible, followed by a loud hiccup. "Off to Italy," he finished with a single sniffle as his own eyes began to water.

"Not yet, *Tio*. You're not getting rid of me that quickly," Rene responded, also rising from the bench to face her uncle with a smile.

"*Oye*, Julia! You killed her already!" Tomás joked, looking at the skeleton outlines painted on Rene's face. Julia rolled her eyes and grunted in annoyance.

"Yes, and you'll be next if you don't get out of here!" Julia warned Tomás as she stepped towards him with intimidation, her hands balled up in fists. Tomás' eyes widened and suddenly ran out of the room laughing like a child just as Javier walked in. "What's going on over here?" Javier questioned playfully with amusement.

"Nothing, *Corazon*. Rene is ready now," Julia replied, motioning at their daughter, who was placing her bag strap over her head and across her shoulder before facing Javier.

"Great. Well done, *Amor*. The makeup looks great. I would have liked less red on the lips, but, I guess this is a special occasion," Javier commented as nicely as possible, crossing his arms against his chest.

"I'd say so, *Papi*. Too much red," Rene agreed, walking towards her father at the door. Julia rolled her eyes, annoyed with their comments on her artwork yet again, slapping her hands against her thighs in frustration.

"Arturo is ready to go too, so, shall we?" Javier petitioned, holding his arm out for Rene. Rene nodded with a smile as she weaved her hand into Javier's arm.

As the two walked out the front door of the *posada*, Tomás was there talking to the horses and Arturo while holding onto the reins for balance. Rene kissed her Nana Maria on the cheek goodbye at the door and hopped up into the driver's box of the wagon next to Javier.

Arturo had come to Puebla for the *Dia de los Muertos* events, just as he promised Ana he would. This was also pleasing to Rene, as she saw it as a sign that he kept his word coming all this way. Ana hadn't much success in the past picking people worthy of her time, when it came to males anyway. Arturo was a little older than the girls. He was 20 years old to be exact and worked at the docks in Veracruz loading and unloading ships. He was fair-skinned and had light brown hair, a younger version of Mr. Lombardi it seemed in a way. Arturo was half native to this land and half German from his father's side, giving him the last name Fein.

As Arturo sat nervously in the back of the wagon, he clutched onto a bouquet of flowers he had bought for Ana, inspecting their quality. Rene also saw this as a good sign for a man like Arturo, showing both excitement and nervousness to see her friend that night. Ana had usually picked more of the cocky types before now. It seemed like her taste in the opposite sex had improved thankfully. Just as Javier commanded the horses to go with a "hiyah!" Arturo finally broke his silence.

"Thank you again, *Señor* Reyes, for letting me be a guest in your home!" Arturo called out over the sounds of the horses' hooves clomping along the clay road along with the wagon's usual creaking sounds. Ana had helped Arturo secure his room at the Reyes' *posada*, of course, for the few days he'd be visiting Ana in town. The Reyes' were happy to accommodate him.

"It's our pleasure, Arturo. Ana is like another daughter to me. *Mi casa es su casa*," Javier replied back to Arturo, carefully looking both back at him and forward at the road ahead. Rene sat quietly listening to the conversation as she looked out at the sunset colored sky beyond the trees as they rode into the village. She was wondering what events tonight might have in store, recalling what the past two years were like for her.

"You are quiet today, *Mija*. Much on your mind?" Javier finally muttered, nudging Rene with his elbow gently as he looked down at her next to him.

"Oh, um, Maybe, *Papi*," Rene replied somewhat awkwardly, "but it's nothing serious." Rene was never good at lying to her father, but she did the best she could. She linked her arm with his and smiled as genuinely as possible at Javier.

"Hmmm," Javier grunted quietly, looking over at Rene again who was back to gazing into the distance with a pensive look on her face. He knew something important had to be on her mind, and she wasn't fooling him. He gave her some space to think and didn't press her for more information and hoped the festivities ahead would help take her mind off the serious topics clearly plaguing her. It was her birthday, after all, and maybe the last one she'd have in their hometown for a while. He remained quiet the rest of the ride into town and did his best to enjoy this time with his daughter since their days were also limited by her departure.

As they arrived at their family store where they promised to meet Ana that night, Javier directed the horses to a stop. Rene quickly hopped off the driver's box before Javier could even help her down. *My daughter, the hombre*, Javier thought, shaking his head with a chuckle. As soon as her boots hit the ground, a familiar voice came from behind her as she adjusted her wardrobe.

"Such a lady," Ana snickered as her heeled, clacky shoes came to a stop.

"You know me…" Rene replied knowing who it was as she whipped around on her boot heel to face her friend. They stood outside the shop in the exact spot where they first met all those years ago. "Wow, Ana, new dress?" Rene gasped with hands on her hips smiling back at her friend.

"Yeah, Ma sold some of the animals patients have given her to help me buy it," Ana shared shyly but still stood confidently in Rene's presence, mouthing "Thank you" in return.

"He'll like it," Rene whispered, cupping the side of her mouth winking at her friend. Ana smiled at Rene just as she remembered something.

"Oh Ren, I almost forgot I wrote this prayer for you! Happy Birthday," she said, pulling out a folded piece of paper from her glove and handed it to Rene. Rene took it from Ana and began to open it when Ana quickly covered the note with her hand and whispered "Wait! You can read it later. No rush!" Rene nodded, carefully putting the paper in her bag.

Rene motioned her head for Ana to follow her around the front of the horses to see Arturo. Ana quickly took a deep breath and fanned her neck with her hand to calm herself as she followed behind Rene. Javier seemed to be finishing a conversation with him as the girls walked up, stopping beside them. Arturo's face quickly changed from serious, to bliss as he spotted Ana. Quickly excusing himself from Javier's presence, he hurried over to Ana, offering her his bouquet of flowers as he bowed with a smile. As Ana and Arturo greeted each other, Rene walked over to Javier to say goodbye.

"I told Arturo I'll come back here around midnight to bring you two home. Should be more than sufficient time for…" Javier looked over at Arturo and Ana holding hands and staring into each other's eyes and breathed, "reunions." He chuckled quietly, shaking his head refocusing on Rene. Rene looked over her shoulder at her friend and her date and shrugged with a smile.

"Ok, *Papi*. We'll see you later," Rene confirmed with her father, kissing him on the cheek and turning to usher her friends towards the excitement in the plaza.

Javier watched the three of them walk off into the crowd before entering the shop to grab a few things at Julia's request before returning home.

As the group cut through the crowds, Rene's mind began to silence the multitude of thoughts swirling inside her and focused on the festivities of the town. Ana had shared that Cristiana would be performing with her *Folklorico* dance group soon at the stage, so they made their way in that direction. Ana was doing her best to be prim and proper as she walked with Arturo, her arm linked in his. When they arrived in the audience area, Ana finally opened up.

"At least one of the Lombardi girls got some rhythm after all," Ana joked to Arturo and Rene. Arturo smiled in response, as Rene snorted and choked on her spit holding back one of her mother's booming laughs. Ana and Arturo looked at Rene with concern, but she waved them off, wheezing that she was okay, when she spotted Charlie in the distance. He was standing on the ledge of the central fountain gazing over the crowd as if he were looking for someone, that someone, of course, being Rene. As her eyes focused on him while still following Ana, he finally gazed in her direction. Spotting her in return, he smiled and lept down, making his way through the crowd to get near Rene. As he approached, Rene became uncertain if it were Charlie, asking Ana if it were him since he was so dressed up. Ana got on her tiptoes and agreed it was him. He politely cut through the crowds, excusing himself as he passed.

"Woah, he cleans up!" Ana suddenly hollered looking back over at Rene, as the band suddenly stopped playing and Charlie reached them. Rene looked mortified.

"Thanks, Ana." Charlie said bashfully looking at Ana before looking at Rene.

Charlie looked like a million bucks. The jet black *charro* with white and gold details sewn across his shoulders and down the breast of his jacket were intricate and dazzling in the lights from the lampposts. His black boots shined like mirrors were brand new too, not to mention he'd gotten a haircut and slicked it back for the occasion. A dark red handkerchief, also weaved with gold threads, stood out around his neck against the bright white color of his new dress shirt underneath.

"Good evening, Rene," Charlie turned to Rene, bringing his arm across his waist and bowed as gentlemanly as possible, looking up with a smile. Rene cleared her throat as quietly as possible to greet Charlie in return.

"Good evening, Charlie," Rene replied with a small curtsy. "This is Arturo, Ana's date." Rene motioned to Arturo, who quickly reached out to shake Charlie's hand. The two greeted each other kindly and returned their attention to the girls when Ana chimed in.

"Ren, we are going to get some food before Cristiana goes up... Will you be right here?" Ana asked as she and Arturo started backing away into the crowds. Rene nodded in return, as Ana disappeared into the sea of people around them.

"You look great, Rene," Charlie chimed in, trying to get Rene's attention away from Ana's departure as he looked her over from head to toe. She wore a long, dark, red-layered skirt with a ruffled fringe. Her white and gold sash cinched a black flowy blouse around her waist to show her figure. The blouse's lace fabric sleeve caps sat just off her shoulders, allowing her long hair to flow against her bare shoulders. Half of her mane was pinned up with a single white rose. Rene finally focused on Charlie hesitantly, as if looking at him were going to make the guard she had put up emotionally come crashing down. She remained poised and took a deep breath.

"Oh, thank you, Charlie," Rene replied humbly. "You.. you're looking fancy yourself tonight," she added with a smile, placing her hand against her stomach to also calm herself and her mixed emotions she had inside. She remembered that even evil had its ways of appearing desirable, and she did her best to fight it.

"*Gracias*, Rene. I saved up from working in the summer... Aunt Emma dressed it up a bit," Charlie shared, looking over his jacket making sure everything was still in place. He felt unsure because of the slight awkwardness that Rene tried hard not to project. He could sense it.

"I see. She is a seamstress of great skill," Rene added, looking at the details of his jacket before glancing back up at his face. "Did my uncle cut your hair again?" She inquired as her eyes looked over the sides of his ears around the top of his head and back into his eyes. She wasn't sure if Charlie grew taller or if it were the boots he was wearing, but he seemed much taller than she remembered before tonight.

"Ah yes, a skilled barber he has turned out to be," Charlie chuckled as he nervously ran his fingers along the side of his head and down the back of his neck. Rene noticed a light mist of sweat escaping through his fingers as he did this.

Jacket must be warm, Rene told herself.

The foursome reunited and made their way as a group closer towards the stage where Cristiana was performing. Ana and Arturo carried their trays of food, eating as politely as possible as they watched the show. Before the dance ended, Dr. Rameriz and Mr. Lombardi met up with their daughter and greeted Arturo formally for the first time. As Rene glanced over at Ana periodically, she noticed that Ana had never looked as happy and content as she did at this moment. A sense of relief came over Rene in regards to Ana as she told herself, *She's gonna be ok.*

When the show was over and Ana's parents headed home with Cristiana, the band started up again. Arturo quickly asked Ana to dance, assuring her he wouldn't let her fall when she warned about her clumsy feet.

"I got you," he whispered gently in Ana's ear. She nodded, affirming she trusted him as he suddenly whisked her off onto the dance floor. Charlie looked over at Rene who had been watching Ana and Arturo take off on to the dance floor, looking happy for her friend as he mustered up the nerve to ask her to dance.

"I'd love to dance with you, Rene, if I may?" Charlie finally asked, just loudly enough for Rene to hear. He was unaware that she could hear a pin drop against the floor, even with the band playing as loudly as it was. Rene looked over at Charlie tilting her head to the side giving him a skeptical look.

"Wh.. what is it?" Charlie stammered as he looked at Rene and then around him, worried.

"Promise you won't crush my toes or something?" she finally answered, glaring into his eyes with a smirk across her lips. Charlie laughed loudly, slapping his thigh with his hand.

"Rene, I told you about my aunts. I've probably danced more than you have," he replied confidently. Rene stood quickly and looked down at Charlie as she thrust her gloved hand out inches from his face causing him to raise his brows in surprise.

"Prove it," Rene challenged him sharply.

Charlie smiled with the corner of his mouth as his brows relaxed. He confidently stood grabbing Rene's hand, lifting it suddenly, taking her into a spin quickly on the dance floor. Suddenly redirecting her back to him, bringing her in close against his chest, meeting her free hand with his. Their fingers aligned. Rene was shocked. Her eyes looked into Charlie's quickly and his into hers before looking down at her lips. Rene's eyes did the same as Charlie grinned brightly, exhaling slowly from his nose. She quickly pushed herself away against his hand to continue the dance, and Charlie did not disappoint.

As Rene was led around the dance floor, even Ana and Arturo were distracted by them as they brushed by. They moved perfectly in unison, as if they had been dancing together for years.

"Ren's good at everything…" Ana shared with Arturo as they went by, shaking her head in disbelief.

"Charlie's pretty good too. He's got me beat, that's for sure," Arturo added, looking back into Ana's eyes.

"Shhhh!!!" Ana replied as she went in for a kiss, taking Arturo by surprise as he immediately kissed her back. He brought his hand up behind her neck to keep her there longer, forgetting about the dancing going on around them.

After a while, the band slowed down, and Charlie again asked for Rene to dance, and she obliged. He put his hand around her waist pulling her back towards the middle of the dance area as she held onto her skirt, catching her breath. She had to admit she was having a good time, and she could appreciate the exercise.

"Thank you for tonight, Rene. I haven't enjoyed myself this much since… I can't remember when." Charlie shared gently as they slowly danced with the sounds of the violin's song in the band. Charlie's mind suddenly drifted back to a time dancing wildly with his mother in their home, not long before her death. He had just turned ten. Shaking off the memory, he refocused on Rene.

"You held up to your word, Charlie. My toes were spared tonight," Rene replied with a smile, as she placed her hand on his arm. Rene suddenly sensed Charlie's heartbeat getting stronger as they continued to dance slowly. His embrace grew stronger, bringing Rene closer, causing their cheeks to touch. This contact suddenly threw Rene out of the moment. An image of Charlie quickly flashed through her mind. He kept repeating something as he stood in a trance in the center of a graveyard. His back was towards her when he quickly turned to face her. His eyes were pits of darkness, and a menacing grin was across his face.

As Rene came back to reality, she suddenly realized that Charlie had pulled away from her cheek and was coming in for a kiss. Rene quickly planted her face into his shoulder to avoid it.

"I can't," She muttered, rejecting him as she took a deep breath to calm herself before carefully pushing herself away from him. Charlie was crushed.

"I tried," Charlie replied as his arms hung disappointedly at his sides. His eyes suddenly went black. Taking a step back, he quickly turned and forced his way through the dance floor, pushing people aside in anger before taking off into the night.

Just then, another image shot through Rene's mind. The graveyard floor was shaking as red, illuminated dry bones began to rise up around Charlie's feet.

"REN!" Ana hollered, shaking Rene from her trance. Rene quickly looked up from the floor and over at Ana standing in front of her. Her arms had been hanging loosely at her sides causing people to think she was just really depressed her date had abandoned her on the dance floor but Ana knew better. As Rene came to, she looked Ana in the eyes. "Your eyes, Ren!" Ana whispered frantically, her mouth half closed, trying not to cause any more of a scene. Rene's eyes were lit in gold for the first time, as she noticed the reflection looking back into Ana's eyes. Rene quickly shielded her eyes, looking back at the ground.

"I gotta go help Charlie," Rene quickly whispered back to Ana.

"Then go!" Ana urged her friend with a shove. Rene took off in Charlie's direction knowing exactly where he was going, grabbing her bag along the way. Ana quickly returned to Arturo and chortled, "She got something in her eye. She'll be ok." She gave him a reassuring smile and led him in the opposite direction, linking her arm in his again. As they left the dance floor, Ana looked back in Rene's direction, worried for her friend. It was 11:00.

    Rene darted after Charlie but held back from going at full speed though as she thought of a plan of action for the task ahead. She held onto the strap of her bag to keep it from swinging as she ran when something scratched at her arm from inside it, beginning to distract her. She stopped to see what it was. It was the letter from Ana.

The prayer, Rene reminded herself as she unfolded the paper to read it.

> Fearless and Bold, they are both.
> Honest and fair, it is declared.
> Wise and steadfast, caring the most.
> Sent from above, we're perfectly paired.
> Patient and understanding are thee,
> a great friend given to me.
>
> Protection from above and guarded below, Lord watch over my friend against any foe.
>
> Restore anything lost or taken, Lord revive a good spirit should it fall into woe.
> Amen.
> Thank you for being my friend Ren.

She quickly read it, feeling empowered. She smiled, folded it back up, and stuck it back in her bag, along with her gloves. She took off running for the cemetery as her eyes gleamed in gold again, feeling them change this time.

As Rene approached the cemetery, she stepped lightly and stealthily, even in her boot clad feet. Charlie was standing there in complete darkness in the center of the cemetery with his arms stretched out and palms face down. At this point in the night, not even the moonlight shone down to light up anything as it hid behind clouds, and the candles brought into the cemetery were all put out. The air grew thick and cold as Rene got closer to the gates. All her senses heightened, and the scent of ash filled the air. Finally, Charlie began to mutter under his breath in an ancient language. Rene focused intently, and she made out what he was chanting after the third time he repeated it.

"The forgotten, awake," she whispered out loud, giving away her position to Charlie as he quickly looked back in her direction. His eyes were pits of darkness, and a menacing grin crossed his face as he spotted her, just as her vision had shown her earlier.

Dammit, Rene, she told herself, shaking her head in disappointment.

"You're in time for the reunion, Rene," Charlie's lips spoke, but a voice not belonging to him came from within him as he turned to make his way towards her. Rene quickly assessed her surroundings in the cemetery. "Don't worry, I showed them the way out already," 'Charlie' spoke again, assuming she was looking for other mourners in the vicinity and continued, "No one was hurt… yet," the spirit hissed, followed by a low cackle. Rene's face grew angry now, not breaking her stare from Charlie as he stared back at her.

"Anything else, Charlie?" Rene inquired, as she began to side step to the right, hoping to draw Charlie out of the center of the cemetery. The demon became bothered upon hearing Charlie's name, breaking a sweat across Charlie's brow signaling a disruption within. He used the sleeve of his jacket to wipe the perspiration from his forehead and then his chin. Its eyes were still locked on Rene.

"They're on their way…" the spirit added angrily, motioning at the ground below him as Rene kept circling to the right, causing the spirit to grow suspicious.
"It's getting hot around here," Rene commented loudly. "Maybe you should take off that jacket Charlie." The spirit broke its eye contact with her and looked down at its sleeve as Rene took off in his direction, charging him at full speed. She quickly stepped

up onto a tombstone and dove at him. As they collided, Rene gripped the collar of Charlie's coat as they tumbled across the floor. As soon as they stopped, Rene quickly planted her knee into his chest and grabbed his wrists with her bare hands pinning him to the ground. When she looked down at Charlie, her hands began to burn against his wrists, causing him to throw his head back and grunt in pain, quickly followed by a deep breath.

"Look who's coming around…" The demon snarled at Rene as his strength suddenly fluxed, causing his arms to grow, ripping his shirt and fitted jacket at the seams. He quickly tumbled onto Rene, straddling her stomach, his hands now holding her wrists against the ground, looking down at her, grinning demonically. The demon's eyes suddenly flashed from their blackness to Charlie's hazel for a moment.

Rene began to struggle to get up when suddenly, her eyes flashed bright white light into the spirit's eyes, blinding him for a moment. Rene swiftly threw Charlie off of her as he covered his eyes, tumbling her body back over her head to face him again. Charlie stood and stumbled side to side, running into tombstones, breaking them as he collided with them. He shook his head vigorously and finally refocused on Rene, breathing heavily. He charged her as he tore off the rest of his shirt and jacket that hung from his neck. Rene swiftly made her way around Charlie's advance, kicking her legs upward, cartwheeling over his shoulder, and launched off his back with a kick. He was thrust downward from her blow. His face planted into the dirt, breaking his nose. He quickly found a fallen branch near his hand and turned to face Rene again, breathing heavily as blood ran down his nose.

"Time to go home, friend," Rene called out to Charlie, getting into her fighting stance.

"I am home," the spirit snapped back as it charged at Rene.

The fight ensued between Charlie and Rene, as she did her best to anticipate his moves and got away by the skin of her teeth. He was fast, almost as fast as she was. However, a spirit of clarity had descended onto Rene, helping her to fight more mentally than physically and it was helping her succeed, when suddenly the bells of the *Catedral* rang in the distance.

Midnight. Rene told herself as she made her way across the graveyard, leaving Charlie heaving for air in the opposite corner.

"Tired yet, Charlie?" she hollered out as Charlie straightened himself up standing there in his trousers and boots. Trancelike, he walked to the center of the cemetery, ignoring Rene's question.

"Time to finish what we started," the demon spoke from inside Charlie without moving his lips.

Rene looked at Charlie confused as she thought of what to do next. Charlie looked worn out, bloodied, and bruised by both Rene and his own actions and didn't appear to be in control of himself.

Cast out the darkness, Rene thought quickly. Her eyes widened, and the candles around the cemetery lit at once.
"You can't help me. It's too late," he called out to Rene. Charlie's spirit had finally come forward. "Get out of here!" he hollered as he clawed at his heart, and the ground began to shake.

"Can't! You're gonna have to let go." Rene replied sternly, watching Charlie begin the fight with the demon inside him. The many church bells clanged in the distance.

"Everyone leaves!" Charlie shouted back, as he fell to his knees with his hands around his neck as if he were going to choke the demon out. Being left alone was one of Charlie's deepest fears with both his mother and father being 'gone.'

"I'm not going anywhere!" Rene called out again, as the sounds of shrieks and cries began to come out of the ground. Time suddenly seemed to stop and Rene's necklace began to warm against her skin. She reached up to hold it and took a deep breath when Ana's prayer came to mind. She closed her eyes and recalled the words quickly. As she finished reciting Ana's words, the tiny sound of a bird chirp caused her to open her eyes that had transitioned to the electric like, gold color again.

It was Reina in ethereal form, lit in bright light. Rene gasped in surprise as Reina swooped down to Rene and gently bounced on her shoulder, chirping just as she used to long ago. Regrouping her thoughts, Rene looked over at Charlie again as a shadow emerged from his side, still connected at his hips, the two slashing at each other as bones began to rise from the ground. Red light also began to emerge from below the demon and Charlie as they fought, getting brighter as time continued to stand still.

Rene looked back at Reina on her shoulder, causing her to take flight. Circling above Rene, the little bird flew wildly, chirping frantically when suddenly flocks of more birds in ethereal form came in from the four corners of the cemetery. In unison, they all charged towards the demon connected to Charlie, as did Rene. As they came to a head, the flock quickly turned heavenward, lifting the demon away from Charlie as Rene tackled him, finally parting him from the demon. He fell lifeless onto his side out of her arms as she tumbled away.

The demon screamed as the birds came cascading back in a downward spiral, suddenly crashing through the shaking floor of the cemetery. They turned the red light to blue as they dissipated into the ground in waves. Time seemed to resume as the final ring of the bells began to fade. Rene looked on in bewilderment at the ground beside Charlie's feet, watching the birds disappear when she suddenly got up and darted at the birds, remembering Reina was among them. She dove so quickly and desperately at the ground in hopes to hold Reina once more that she landed hard on her chin knocking herself out.

As her eyes closed, the cemetery went pitch black, stilled and silenced all at once.

Epilogue

November 2, 1901 12:07am

"Ren isn't here!" Ana called out breathlessly at Javier as she and Arturo ran towards the wagon.

"Where is she?" Javier replied sternly, but clearly concerned for his daughter's whereabouts.

"She went after Charlie… she didn't come back," Ana heaved as she stood by the driver's box, looking up at Javier. Arturo rubbed her back nervously as he looked around, hoping Rene would show up as they had planned earlier.

Javier's brow perplexed as he thought for a moment, nodded, and instructed the two to quickly get on board. His daughter was always on time, and he needed to find her. Arturo quickly lifted Ana into the wagon, and by the time Arturo's feet left the ground, Javier shouted for the horses to head out. Ana frantically scrambled to Javier's side of the wagon as he made his way through the dim back streets of Puebla, avoiding the *Dia de los Muertos* crowd still gathering in the village center.

"Her eyes were gold, *Señor* Reyes!" Ana whispered loudly enough for Javier to hear as she steadied herself in the moving wagon.

Javier's own eyes grew wide as he looked back at his daughter's friend for a moment. He nodded in acknowledgement at Ana and replied, "HOLD ON!" cracking the reins to hurry the horses along faster. Ana fell back in the wagon onto Arturo who was ready to receive her.

"I got you," Arturo whispered as he helped Ana onto the seat beside him. Ana cracked a smile as her eyes grew watery, worried about her friend.

As Javier arrived at the cemetery and brought the horses to an abrupt stop, and quickly dismounted the driver's box. He hustled towards the swarm of people chattering and observing something in the center of the grounds.

"*Pardone, pardone!*" Javier called out as he pushed through the onlookers, while Ana and Arturo followed closely behind. "Rene!" Javier hollered, as he found his daughter lying on the ground near Charlie. He fell to his knees as he grabbed his daughter's shoulders and brought her into his arms and towards his chest. Ana gasped, bringing her hands to her mouth as she saw her lifeless looking friend. Arturo made his way to Charlie's side, quickly turning him over onto his back.

"Oh no!" Ana called out as she began sobbing, seeing Charlie's bloodied nose and bruised body in the moonlight. Arturo leaned in towards Charlie's nose to check if he were still breathing.

"He's alive!" he called out, quickly removing his own jacket and covering Charlie's bare chest.

"*Papi...?*" Rene finally responded, slowly opening her eyes as she looked up at her father.

"*Sí, Amor*. It's me," Javier sighed, bringing his daughter in for a hug.

Ana quickly went to Rene's side and grabbed her hand and brought it to her face, sniffling in between sobs. "Ren! You're awake. Thank God!" she gasped, finally smiling at her friend.

"Charlie…?" Rene uttered softly.

"He's breathing, but… he's not waking up," Ana quickly replied with another sniffle.

"We better get your mama then," Rene urged with a grunt as she began to move her legs to stand up. Javier stood and helped his daughter rise. Rene looked over at Charlie and back to her father. "Maybe we need Esther too," she finished.

To Be Continued…

Coming Soon

REN: The Revival

About the Author
& Illustrator

Christina M. Garcia spent over 15 years in real estate sales, marketing, and development before stepping into her calling as a storyteller and illustrator. She holds a degree in computer graphic design and has been an avid journalist of personal and family life stories since she was a teenager. After spending 25 years journaling and learning about personal growth and development, she shares stories based on real life events, experiences, and wisdom to teach to the next generation, fulfilling her desire to make a difference in the world. Christina is a family woman living in Southern California.